# Red Echo

## *A Tale of Two Sisters*

Monique Elise

ISBN: 1732075751
ISBN-13: 978-1-7320757-5-7

*This novel is dedicated to the loving memory of my wonderful uncle, Carnell "Junebug" Talford Jr. I will love and miss you forever, please give Aunt Robin a hug and kiss for me.*

# ACKNOWLEDGMENTS

To my fabulous readers, I love you all! Thank you for continuing to take this journey with me. Can you believe that this is book number four? Stay tuned, because I'm only getting warmed up!

XOXO - Monique Elise

# CONTENTS


| | |
|---|---|
| Chapter One | 1 |
| Chapter Two | 11 |
| Chapter Three | 22 |
| Chapter Four | 30 |
| Chapter Five | 42 |
| Chapter Six | 51 |
| Chapter Seven | 58 |
| Chapter Eight | 64 |
| Chapter Nine | 75 |
| Chapter Ten | 82 |
| Chapter Eleven | 95 |
| Chapter Twelve | 103 |
| Chapter Thirteen | 113 |
| Chapter Fourteen | 121 |
| Chapter Fifteen | 129 |
| Chapter Sixteen | 136 |
| Chapter Seventeen | 144 |
| Chapter Eighteen | 156 |
| Chapter Nineteen | 160 |
| Chapter Twenty | 164 |
| Coming Soon | 185 |
| More Books | 192 |
| About Monique | 194 |

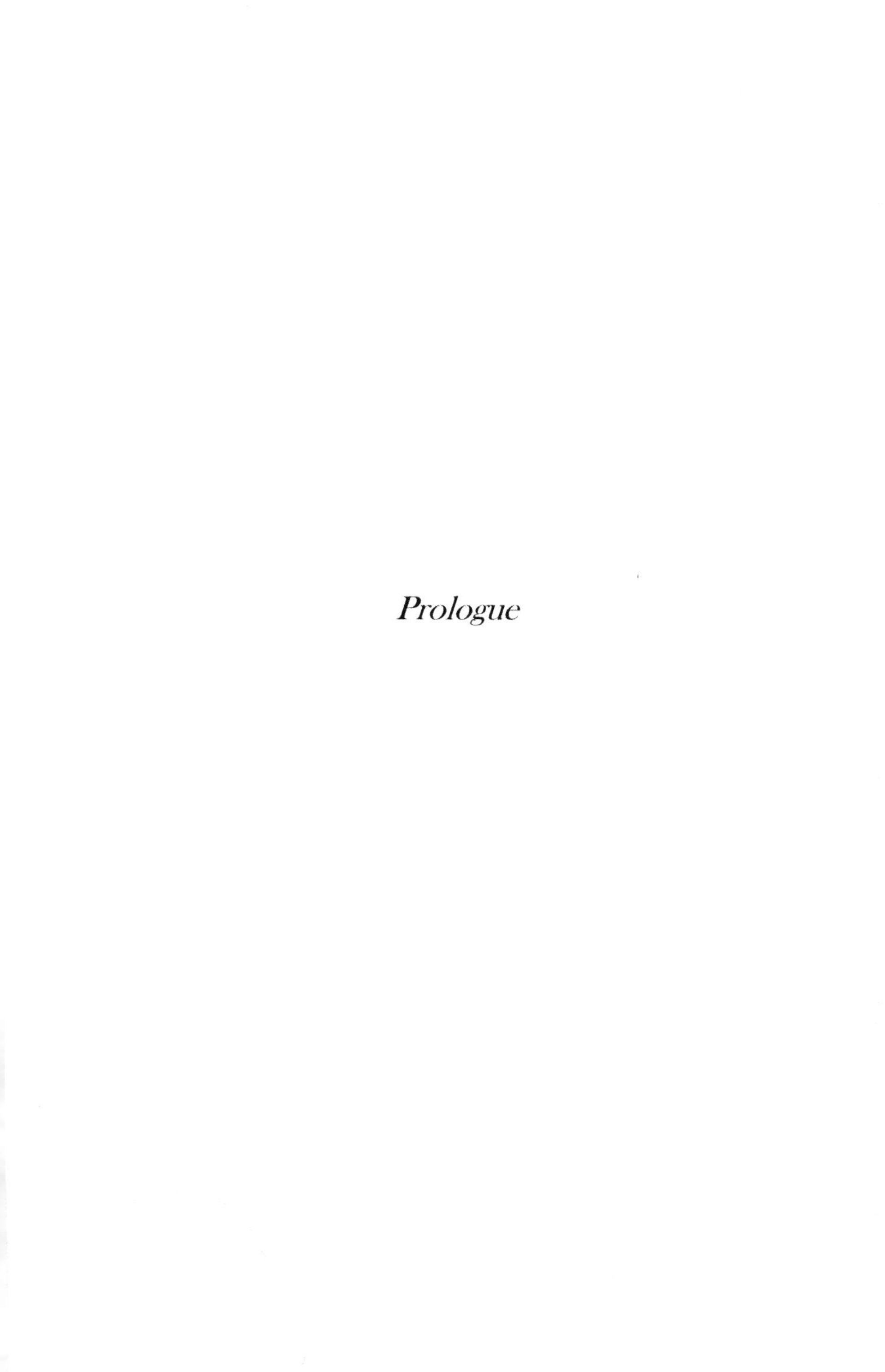

# *Prologue*

*Thursday, February 14, 2020*

*Her slaps and kicks do little to slow him down. A sense of overwhelming panic fills her body as his steel-like hands tightly close in around her neck, making it nearly impossible to breathe. His black eyes are menacing and cold as they pierce through her soul, sending chills down her spine. Despite the terror she feels, she refuses to give up. She doesn't want to die, not like this.*

Her breathing is heavy and labored. Night terrors like this always leave her feeling on edge. Although she's stuck in a deep slumber, she's somehow aware of how fast her heart is beating and the sensation of pressure weighing her down. The pressure is so immense, she knows that she may sink through her queen-sized mattress at any moment. Her subconscious screams at her, begging her to awaken.

Frustrated, she wills herself to wake up. Her eyes flicker beneath her eyelids, finally opening. As she slowly comes to, she feels hazy and disoriented. Now fully conscious, she's relieved that her bad dream was just that, a dream.

The single flame of a candle casts its soft reflection throughout her bedroom. With sleep still in her eyes, she takes a deep breath and stares up at her high ceiling, listening to the howling wind and pouring rain outside. With little notice, a shadow quickly moves across the wall, taking her completely by surprise. It happens so fast that she isn't completely certain that she even saw it. She sits up and scans her surroundings, but nothing seems to be out of place. Her clothing from the day before is exactly where she tossed it, and her Celine bag is still on top of the dresser where she left it.

Then, she sees it again, this time more clearly. A silhouette of a figure standing in the corner of her bedroom, moving closer and closer.

*Is this too a dream?*

She squints her eyes to better focus. But as the figure slowly comes forward, the hairs on the back of her neck stand at attention. Her heartbeat becomes irregular, and adrenaline kicks into overdrive when she finally realizes this isn't a dream at all. In fact, her worst nightmare is coming true right before her eyes; she's not alone.

*How long have they been there?*

*What do they want?*

The questions swirl in her head, but it's like her fear has snatched her tongue, making it impossible to speak. Fear pumps through her veins, and her eyes dart towards her bedroom door. In a swift movement, she jumps up, preparing to make an escape. But her assailant is lightning fast and by her side at once. She knows she's too late when she feels their fingers tug on her hair, yanking her body back down and onto the bed.

She swings and thrashes, trying to defend herself, but they're seemingly unfazed.

Petrified, she screams, finally finding her voice, "Who are you? Why are you doing this?"

They say nothing.

Then she feels a sharp stinging pain in her side, temporarily incapacitating her. Seconds later when she regains some of her strength, she tries to scream for help. But the roaring thunder drowns out her cries, causing her pleas to fall on deaf ears. She's quickly silenced by a gloved hand placed over her mouth and nose, making it hard for her to breathe. She strikes a few blows and claws away at them. Her determination to fight back ignites a fire deep within, and she refuses to give up. But when she sees the silver glisten of the knife, her heart sinks into the deepest pit of her stomach.

She relentlessly kicks and squirms, trying to fight her way free, but nothing she does stops them from plunging the large knife deep into her chest. It all happens so fast. Before she can make one last attempt to save herself, her attacker places the cold, hard blade to her neck. Hot tears stream down her cheeks as the sharp edge is roughly dragged across her throat.

Her kicking legs slow until they finally stop moving. She feels herself choking on her own blood, as she finally sees the face of her killer. The shock has now consumed her.

*Why?*

She fights to keep her eyes open as she stares into the evil eyes of her killer. Moments later, her life finally slips away with her last breath.

# OLIVIA

*God, please don't let him kill me this time.* My face stings from the impact of his enormous palm coming across my face. Memories of Marcus' voice rings in my head.

*"I'll never hit you again, Olivia."*

*"You're safe with me, I promise."*

I guess that's a thing of the past because now he is seething with fury. Without notice, he reaches for a handful of my hair before punching me in my lower abdomen. The impact takes me by surprise, causing me to crouch over and fall onto the floor, struggling to catch my breath.

"I'm sorry," I pant.

However, if I'm being honest, I don't know what I did to set him off this time. Frankly, I never know what I will do or say to upset him next. Lately, our relationship has left me feeling like I'm stumbling through a minefield, setting off bombs left and right, constantly terrified and anxious about the consequences of my next move.

Unfortunately, tonight is no different. One minute, we were preparing to go to dinner for Valentine's Day. I was getting ready, but I couldn't decide on the right lip color. I tend to be indecisive at times and was torn between a bold crimson-colored lipstick, a gift from my sister, or a subtle mauve-colored lip gloss. He insisted that I wear the lip gloss, suggesting that the red would make me look like a slut. I quickly snorted at his comment, thinking that his logic was ridiculous and that he was only saying those things because he didn't like the person it came from. Then I proceeded to finish getting ready for our date. Next thing I know, my hair was nearly ripped from my skull, and I was being slapped and thrown across my master bedroom.

"You just love making me upset, don't you?" Marcus accuses, interrupting my thoughts.

I cry, unsure of what to say.

"Why do you insist on making me the bad guy, Liv?" he questions.

"I'm sorry, I won't do it again," I vow.

"You always say that shit, yet here we are!" Marcus says, hovering over me.

I instinctively curl up in a fetal position, keeping my head down in shame. His feet furiously trek back and forth in front of me. My heart races, fearful of what he is planning to do next and praying for an escape from my own personal hell. Gradually, I hear his steps slow down as each silent moment passes between us.

Droplets of blood mixed with snot escape my nose, and I quickly wipe them away with the back of my hand. He approaches me once more, the rage in his eyes has transformed into a look of tenderness in mere seconds. He hands me a tissue before helping me to my feet. Marcus pulls me in close, visibly pained by what he's just done. The rollercoaster of his emotions gives me whiplash.

"I'm sorry, baby, I'll do a better job working on my temper," he says.

I want to refute his words. I've heard this too many times to truly believe it. But if I deny him, I know that'll only upset him again. So, I nod my head in agreement instead to keep the peace.

Marcus gently cups my face, "I love you so much, Olivia. I just don't want anyone to look at you and get the wrong impression, you know? You're the most beautiful woman I've ever seen. You're an angel, my angel."

He stares deeply into my eyes with each word he recites. There it is, that look. The look that keeps me stuck in this whirlwind of a relationship, fearing for my life more often than I should. My mother would always tell my sister and me that loving the wrong man can be dangerous or even get you killed. I know that I have to get out, and soon, otherwise, I'll end up dead.

~

It's been two days since our Valentine's Day blow up. I woke up this morning, grateful to have some solace. But lately, two days is a long stretch of peace in this house. Deep down, I know that it will only be a matter of time before Marcus explodes again.

Well, today is that day. Marcus didn't take too kindly to our mailman greeting me by my first name and wishing me well. Somehow our innocent and friendly exchange translated to an affair, according to Marcus. He accused me of sleeping around. And against my better judgment, I let him know how absurd he was being. It was like he transformed into the Hulk right in front of my eyes. Marcus held nothing back when he punched me in my face and then choked me until I nearly passed out.

My eye throbs from the assault. Defeated, I stare at my fresh bruise in the mirror. I feel sickened by what I see. The luster of my black hair has faded; my eyes look weary and tired, and my almond brown skin is drab and dull. The woman staring back at me is a complete stranger, someone I don't know.

It's been three hundred and ninety-four days since I uprooted my life and moved to Charlotte to be with this man. Sadly, I've already lost count of the number of times Marcus has put his hands on me, degraded and humiliated me. To make matters worse, I'm all alone in this city, over five hundred miles away from my home, Philadelphia, living in a nightmare and no one knows. My friends and family think that I've found the love of my life, living the fairytale, but that couldn't be further from the truth. No one knows my secret, not even my twin sister, London.

*I can't do this anymore.*

Feeling lost and in need of a familiar voice, I reach for my phone and dial my sister's number. It's been days since we last talked, but I can't shake feeling that she needs me just as much as I need her right now. I had a dream about her two nights before and I can't seem to shake the feeling that she's in trouble. My heart sinks by the sixth unanswered ring. Quickly after, I am greeted by her voicemail.

"Hey, you know who this is! Sorry that I missed your call. I'm probably busy living my life, you should try it. Bye."

*Beep!*

"Lon, it's Liv," I sob. "I need you, please call me back when you get this."

I know that she will be by my side the moment she hears my message. However, I also know that once I reveal the truth about my relationship, my sister will hold nothing back in expressing her disapproval of Marcus and our relationship. She wasn't exactly thrilled when I told her I was moving away to be with him. In fact, she was against it from the beginning. It was the furthest apart we'd ever been in our lives. I know deep down that she was disappointed and felt like I'd allowed a man to come between us. None of that matters anymore. I can't keep this a secret any longer. I need a way out. I need my sister's help.

Sometimes I wish that I could be as fearless and unapologetic as London. Although we're identical, when it comes to love and life in general, we couldn't be more different. She prides herself on her ability to be independent and refuses to be tied down by anyone. London sees most men as a means to an end and never allows herself to get too attached. She has this uncanny ability to string any man she sees fit along until they're eating out of the palm of her hand. I, on the other hand, have a much more conventional idea of love and the way I relate to the opposite sex. But as it turns out, I must've gone about it all wrong. It seems that my desire to be loved and find my prince charming has led me right into the arms of a monster.

A soft knock on the bathroom door snaps me back into reality.

"Olivia, I'm sorry. Open the door," Marcus begs.

I take a deep breath.

"I need a moment," I call out.

He knocks again, this time with more force, "Let me in."

"Why? So that you can hit me again?" I challenge him.

Frustrated, I splash some cool water onto my face and turn my back towards the mirror, leaning against the granite countertop. I look down and see the shadows of his feet pacing under the crack of the doorframe.

Marcus orders, "Open the fucking door!"

"Or what? Are you going to bust the door down? Leave me alone. I'm sick of this Marcus," I reveal.

My heart sprints, and my knees shake, preparing for another fight.

Suddenly, there is a loud thud at the door, causing it to tremble. Then again, this time louder and more forceful than before. My stomach sinks with the realization that he's actually trying to break the door down. I panic, my eyes frantically searching the bathroom. In an instant, a set of brass candle-holders grabs my attention, a housewarming gift from Lon. I'm relieved to know that she's here for me, even when she isn't physically.

The door shakes again. I quickly scurry across the bathroom and reach up to retrieve the largest candle-holder of the two, carefully placing the unused candle down onto the shelf. I inhale deeply to calm my nerves and wait silently by the door, prepared to defend myself.

Just as I do, Marcus bursts through the bathroom like he's a defensive tackle, causing the door panel to splinter into pieces. As he enters, I swiftly swing the candle-holder clear across his skull with all of my might, causing him to fall to the ground. Stunned, he grabs the back of his head, which is now bleeding, before turning to look at me.

"You bitch!"

I can see the wrath in his dark green eyes. My skin grows hot with panic. I know that if he gets his hands on me, he will have every intention of making me pay for what I've just done. And I know that if he succeeds, he is going to kill me. The thought horrifies me, causing me to snap. I can't let him hurt me anymore. I strike him again and again, this time, causing ruby red blood to spray across our white shower curtain and tiled floor. Just when I feel like my arms are about to give out, his body goes limp, and he stops moving.

I freeze in place, my chest heaving from the adrenaline.

"Marcus," I whisper.

No answer.

I say his name a little more loudly this time, "Marcus."

Silence.

I use my foot to softly kick his leg, nothing. Still in disbelief, I drop down to my knees and scoot closer to him. I carefully lean over him, trying to listen for his breathing. My palms sweat when I hear nothing. Finally, I slowly reach out my hand, placing two fingers at the base of his neck, feeling for a pulse. But there isn't one.

*He's dead.*

The realization makes my head spin. I feel myself becoming distressed and quickly go into damage control. My murder weapon still in hand, I grasp my phone and stuff it into my back pocket before running into our bedroom. Once there, I reach for my overnight bag, wrap the candle-holder in an old pillowcase before stuffing it inside. Then I hurry towards my closet and snatch whatever clothing I can find. I reach up to the closet's top shelf, trying to grab my sneakers to put them on. As I do, about six other shoe boxes fall to the floor causing a mixture of mine and Marcus' shoes to be displaced. I gasp when I see three thick wads of cash in between our pile of shoes.

I pick them up and inspect them, all hundred and fifty-dollar bills. Without giving it a second thought, I throw the money into my bag before putting on my running sneakers, retrieving my purse, keys and dash out of the house.

In a flash, I toss my bags into the backseat of my silver Volkswagen before hopping into the front seat and throwing my car into drive. Tightly gripping the steering wheel, I pull out of my driveway and speed down the street. Every few seconds, I look into my rearview mirror, watching the life that I knew grow smaller and smaller in the distance.

A few minutes pass, and I find myself driving with nowhere to go. I can't hold it in any longer. I pull my car over and let the tears stuck in the middle of my throat come up to the surface. The pure adrenaline I'd once felt has subsided, and the reality of everything that happened finally settles in.

*Oh my god! I killed him.*

*What am I going to do?*

*Where am I going to go?*

*Should I turn myself in?*

*It was self-defense; they can't charge me; he abused me.*

My heart sinks when I realize that although that was, in fact, true, I failed to ever get the police involved or document any of the incidents and all that Marcus subjected me to. I curse myself for my stupidity and instinctively pound my fist into the dashboard.

*I know better than to let this happen!*

*How could I be so stupid in love?*

As the tears continue to stream down my face, I resign to turning myself in. I shift my car back into drive and head in the direction of the police station. The thumping of my heart gets faster and more profound with each streetlight that I pass. I can see the signs for the station in the distance, and my palms grow sweaty causing me to pull over on the side of the road again.

*It was self-defense.*

But before I can wallow in my sorrows and face the consequences, my cell rings, causing me to jump with surprise. London pops into my head, and I eagerly reach over to the passenger seat to pick my phone up. I need her now more than ever.

My relief suddenly changes to confusion when her name doesn't come across the screen. This number is unknown. I shrug, maybe she changed numbers again. Nevertheless, I need to talk to her. She'd know what to do in this situation.

"Hello, Lon?" I answer.

"Is this Olivia Burrows?" an unfamiliar male voice comes through the receiver.

I sit up in my driver's seat, "Yes, who is this?"

"My name is Brian Andrews. I'm a detective with the Philadelphia Police Department."

"Yes?"

I can sense his apprehension.

"Do you know London Burrows?"

"That's my sister; what's this about?" I ask.

"Ms. Burrows, we believe that we found your sister this morning. I hate to tell you this, but she was murdered two nights ago," he reveals.

My heart stops, and my ears go numb. In a matter of seconds, my world as I've known it has been forever changed.

# LONDON

*Thursday, February 14, 2019*

I walk into the swanky Four Seasons hotel and head straight towards the lounge. My Tom Ford stilettos echo as I make my way across the black marbled floor, passing numerous admirers along the way. One by one, their eyes become fixated on me.

"Dirty martini please," I say to the male attendant, another fan, as I take a seat at the bar.

He eyes me with fervor before smiling and tending to my drink. I tuck my honey-blond colored hair neatly behind my ear, displaying my two-carat diamond earrings. Moments later, the flirty bartender returns, placing my martini down in front of me. I reach into my scarlet leather Yves Saint Laurent clutch to hand him a fifty-dollar bill. But before I can, a black American Express card is handed over.

"A woman this beautiful should never have to pay for a drink," he says with a baritone voice.

I look up and am greeted by a slightly older version of Shemar Moore.

"Porsha?" he asks with an extended hand.

I nod, "And you're Omar."

He nods, visibly pleased, "Yes. It's a pleasure to finally meet you."

Omar leans in, giving me a soft kiss on the cheek, a gentleman, I can tell.

I smile and quickly scan his indigo blue tailor-made suit and shoes. His silver Rolex neatly covers his left wrist. I'm relieved; he's much more handsome than I expected him to be. We spent the last couple of days messaging one another online before we finally decided to meet in person.

Omar, who according to my recent Google search, is Omar Winston. A former banking executive who'd suddenly left the industry and now he was being paid big bucks to consult banks on ways to expand and stay ahead in the emerging market. I can't lie, his work is pretty impressive.

He signals the bartender, "Scotch, neat." Then he turns his attention back towards me, "You're absolutely stunning."

I grab my drink and take a sip, "Thank you, I can tell you're a charmer."

He smiles, "Not lately. All I do is work."

"I take it business is doing well?" I ask.

Local news says that Omar is quickly becoming one of the highest-paid consultants in the city. I know that I've hit the jackpot.

Omar nods, "I guess you can say that."

"You took a break from work to hang with me? I feel so special," I tease.

His cheeks flush a little. I can tell he's slightly nervous.

"It's been a while since I've done this," he admits.

Something, thanks to my slight investigation, I'd already known. This poor guy just went through a pretty nasty divorce. The bartender gently places the scotch down, and Omar takes a sip before focusing his attention back on to me.

"Really? You're so handsome, I'm sure you can have any woman you want," I flirt.

He snorts, "Maybe once upon a time."

I cock my head to the side, "That sounds like there's a story behind it."

"You haven't heard?"

I shake my head, "Honestly, I live in my own little world most of the time."

He laughs, "I don't want to scare you off."

"I'm a big girl," I reassure him.

"Well, I just finalized my divorce a few months back. I had an affair with my employee a few years ago. My wife at the time found out about it. Completely went ballistic, keyed the girl's car and showed up to our hotel one day with a gun. Long story short, she ended up shooting the young lady," he explains.

My eyes grow big, "Are you serious? Oh my goodness!"

I'll never understand women that completely lose their sense over a man. I get feeling upset, but why not just leave? This is the exact reason why I specifically stay away from married men. Divorced, or casually dating is fine. But anyone that's married or separated is a no-go for me. It gets entirely too messy.

He nods, "Luckily her injuries weren't life-threatening, but she didn't want anything more to do with me. Not long after, my wife left too. I deserved what happened to me. I was an awful husband."

I reach out my hand, placing it on his knee, "Hey, we all make mistakes. You live and you learn right?"

He nods, "I royally fucked that up."

"Well, that was then," I say leaning into him, strategically showing my midriff. "You don't need to worry about any of that with me."

Omar softly kisses my hand, "I love that you're so easy to talk to."

I smile once more before finishing off my martini. I know that our night is only beginning.

~

About an hour later, Omar uses his hotel room key to open the door to the room suite. He holds it open for me while gripping the bottle of Dom Perignon we'd just ordered. I make my way into the room and head straight towards the bathroom to reapply my favorite cherry red lipstick. I delicately fluff my hair and adjust my skin-tight dress. Once I'm pleased with what I see, I reenter the room and am greeted by Omar holding out my glass of champagne.

"Thank you," I smile.

We walk over to the velvet gray love chair placed in front of the fireplace and take a seat. I cross my thighs in his direction, inviting him to rest his hands on my long legs.

He holds his glass up for a toast, "Here's to making new friends."

"Cheers."

We tap our glasses and toss our drinks back. Once we finish, I swiftly grab his glass before heading to the bar for a refill.

Before I do, I turn to Omar, "Do you mind putting on some music to set the mood?"

"Not at all," he says with a grin.

"Make it sexy," I order as I pour our champagne.

He chuckles, "Yes mam."

While he's looking through his phone for the perfect selection, I tend to our drinks. Out of the corner of my eye, I see him stand and make his way over to the Bluetooth speaker system by the bed. After a moment, the sultry voice of Maxwell fills the room. Omar removes his suit coat and tosses it onto the bed before approaching me from behind.

He kisses the nape of my neck, "You smell amazing."

"Thank you," I reply.

Passing Omar his drink, I carefully watch him take a long sip as I drink mine. Before he can say another word, I pull him in for a deep kiss. He uses his free hand to caress my body and search for the zipper on my dress. I briefly pull away, turning my back to him, granting easier access and placing our empty glasses down onto the bar counter.

Moments later, he eagerly unzips my black form-fitting dress, helping me step out of it before tossing it to the floor. I turn to face him, revealing my crimson lace lingerie set. He's pleased with the sight of my body.

My hands slightly tug on his silk tie. I lead him to the bed and push him down onto his back. Straddling him, I seductively unbutton his shirt as he reaches for my bra straps, pulling them down over my shoulders. I allow his hands to explore my body, cupping my breasts and gripping my ass. I lean over him kissing him once more, before leaving a trail of kisses all over his body from his collarbone, down to his hard chest, then above the brim of his pants.

I tug on his belt buckle and look up at him, "Tell me what you want."

Omar licks his lips, "I want to feel your mouth on me."

I oblige him, gently taking his cock out and pulling his pants down to his ankles. As I place him into my mouth, I can feel him grow larger and harder with each gripping suck. Before long, Omar pulls me to him, crashing his champagne-flavored tongue with mine and flipping me onto my back. My soft moans sing out over the music as he tenderly licks and kisses my breasts.

He whispers into my ear, "Now, tell me what you want, Porsha."

"I want you inside of me," I pant as my fingers dig into his back with anticipation.

We kiss once more before he pulls away. I watch him as he reaches for his pants and pulls out a golden Magnum condom. My fingers trail down to my lady pearl, and I sensually touch myself as I watch him slide the condom on.

Within seconds, he's back on top of me and places one of my breasts into his mouth. By now I'm dripping wet and ready to feel all of him. I reach down, finding his shaft and eagerly pulling it inside of me, taking him completely by surprise.

I get lost in the sensation and tightly wrap my legs around his waist. The music changes as we become absorbed with one another. My body convulses as Omar completely takes over with each powerful stroke.

Suddenly, he turns me over onto my stomach before pulling on my hips and bringing my ass up in the air.

"Damn," I pant, as he enters me from behind.

Seriously, this guy fucks like a champ. Omar slowly licks and kisses the passion-filled sweat off of my back as he simultaneously reaches around to caress my clit.

I bite my bottom lip, "You're going to make me cum."

He smiles and kisses on my neck, "Cum for me then, baby."

It isn't long before we both explode with orgasms and crash into the king-sized mattress, trying to catch our breath. Thirty or so minutes later, after some more kissing and cuddling, I pull myself up from the bed.

"You're phenomenal," Omar compliments.

I look over my shoulder and smile, "So are you."

I pull my panties on and follow with my dress.

"Can you help me?" I ask, taking a seat beside him on the bed.

He nods and sits up to assist me.

"Would you prefer cash or a check?" he asks once he zips me up.

"Cash will do," I say, before rising up and walking into the bathroom to fix my hair and reapply my lipstick.

Moments later, I rejoin him in the room. He's now standing in his boxers and hands me a white envelope.

"Five hundred an hour, right?" he confirms.

I nod, "Yup."

I quickly count the money and see a little extra in the envelope. I look at him with shock.

Omar winks, "Consider that a tip."

"Thank you," I smile.

"I want to see you again," he says.

"Let me know. I'll be waiting," I reply.

We kiss once more before I grab my purse and head back out into the night.

*Jackpot indeed.*

~

*Thursday, February 28, 2019*

*The only true wisdom is knowing that you know nothing.*

I stare at the words written out on the whiteboard before me and try to discern their true meaning.

My professor stops writing and turns to face us, "Socrates, the infamous Greek philosopher, was the shit."

The thirty or so students in the classroom, including myself, giggle in unison. For the last two and a half years, I've been busting my ass and accelerating my studies. If all goes well, I'll have my Bachelor's degree in Psychology within the next year. My decision to go to school wasn't an easy one. One day, I just woke up and wanted more for myself. Yes, escorting could be fun and extremely lucrative. But I know that this life won't last forever; there's no future in it. I need an exit plan. Getting my degree and starting a real career would be just that.

This class in particular, has quickly become one of my favorites this semester and a highlight of my week, mainly because of Professor Harris. Not only is his class fun, but he's also able to relate to his students in an organic and genuine way. It doesn't hurt that he's easy on the eyes, extremely easy on the eyes.

He chuckles, revealing a subtle dimple in his left cheek before making his way toward his desk in front of the classroom and casually leaning against it, "On a serious note, Socrates was infamous for his ability to question everything in life, something that ultimately got him killed."

I eagerly type some notes into my MacBook before returning my attention back to him.

"Socrates wasn't afraid to debate what others believed. He wasn't fearful of the words 'why' and 'how,' and that pissed a lot of people off. In fact, they accused him of being anti-democratic for simply thinking outside of the box," Professor Harris explains.

He rises back to his feet and coolly walks through the room, placing his hands in the front pocket of his denim jeans, "Last week, I asked you to write about the foundations of critical thinking and how it has pushed mankind forward."

I navigate to my computer's saved documents and open up my paper.

"Now I want to know, why do you think critical thinking and debate are so important for society?" our professor asks.

A few hands go up, and I nervously raise mine as well.

Professor Harris' eyes settle on me, and he smiles, "London, yes, what do you think?"

I explain, "Debate is the foundation of good critical thinking. Healthy conflict and disagreement are necessary for moving science and mankind forward."

He nods, visibly pleased with my answer, "That's correct. Could you imagine what this world would be like if people like Socrates didn't question or challenge anything?"

Class continues, and I give Professor Harris my undivided attention. Before I know it, the class is coming to an end.

But before it does, Professor Harris says, "Don't be afraid to challenge your thinking! For next week, I'd like you to read about Benjamin Libet's 'Free Will Experiment' and write a one-thousand-word essay on the impact of the Split-Mind Strategy. Have a great weekend everyone. I'll see you next week!"

My classmates eagerly gather their belongings and file out of the door. I shut down my laptop and store it into my Louis Vuitton leather tote. As I do, my phone rings, a text from Richard.

**RICHARD: I NEED TO SEE YOU. DINNER TOMORROW, 8 PM?**

I smile and send him a quick text accepting his offer before rising from my seat and making my exit.

"Great job today, London; if you keep this up, you'll finish with top honors in no time," Professor Harris calls out, stopping me.

I blush, excited at my progress, "Thank you so much, Professor Harris."

"Chase," he interrupts. "I'm not that much older than you."

I blush again, feeling a tad embarrassed. I know that I'm one of his older students.

He senses my shame immediately, "Don't do that, everything happens when it's supposed to happen, London. You're an amazing student, and I know that you'll be great at whatever you decide to do. You've got everything it takes, trust me."

I smile at his compliment, "Thank you, I really appreciate that."

Professor Harris smiles, "I'll see you next week."

"See you then," I say before leaving.

# OLIVIA

My eyes are fixated on the road ahead. I drive in complete silence, a million thoughts running rapidly through my mind. It feels like I'm stuck in a bad dream. My sister, my twin, might be dead, murdered.

*Who would do this to her and why?*

As I continue my drive north up I-95, I find myself repeating that question over and over again in my head. Deep down, I'm praying that the police have it wrong, that it's not London and it's somebody else. But she's still not answering my calls, and that's not like her. The realization that I may now truly be alone makes my skin shiver. That soul wrenching thought makes me want to scream and gauge my own eyes out. That, on top of the fact that I've killed a man, makes me nauseous. I can feel myself coming apart at the seams.

Hours later, the Philadelphia skylines look taller than I remember. The city is fast-paced and alive, but I feel dead inside. I pull into the visitor's parking space at the police precinct and adjust my rearview mirror to check myself. I look like shit. My eye is now black and blue, and my bottom lip is slightly swollen. I desperately try making myself look more presentable by pulling my hair up into a ponytail and putting on my oversized sunglasses. Once inside the police station, I approach the officer manning the front desk.

"How can I help you?" he says, barely looking up at me.

"I'm here to see Detective Andrews," I explain.

The officer picks up the phone, quickly dialing a number on the keypad.

"Andrews? Yeah, I've got a woman up here asking for you," he states. "Alright," he says before hanging up.

I nervously fidget, adjusting my black puffer coat.

The officer finally looks in my direction, "Detective Andrews will be right up, feel free to have a seat over in the waiting area."

I nod and head towards the waiting room to sit down. After taking my seat, I watch the clock, counting each second that ticks by. I tap my leg, trying my best to maintain my composure, but I'm hanging on by a thread.

"Ms. Burrows?" a smooth voice asks.

"Yes," I say looking up.

He extends his hand, "Thank you for coming in today. I'm Detective Andrews. We spoke on the phone. I'll be the lead detective in your sister's case."

I stand up to return the gesture and try to be polite. He is tall and handsome; his skin is a deep, mocha brown, and his goatee is neatly trimmed. I can smell the Irish Spring on his skin. Marcus used that soap all the time. The scent makes me want to vomit.

"Umm, where's the bathroom?"

"Right this way," he says, leading me down a busy hallway.

He points me towards the bathroom, two doors down on the left, and I'm quick on my feet. I rush through the restroom door, running into the first open stall, throwing up everything that is sitting in my stomach.

~

I stand on the other side of the large glass mirror alongside Detective Andrews. My heart feels like it's going to burst out of my jacket. Although I can feel the heat coming through the vent in the ceiling, I can't stop shivering. The coroner, a short, silver-haired woman, places her notepad down on a table by the door before walking over to the single table placed in the middle of the metallic, luminescent room. The lights are bright and somewhat blinding. Before removing the long, white sheet, she looks up, awaiting her signal.

"Are you ready?" Detective Andrews asks, turning to me.

I slowly nod, but deep down, I want to run away and never look back.

He gives the coroner the official "ok," and she carefully pulls the sheet back.

There's London, cold and motionless, not a sign of life is left in her body. Her skin is clammy and pale. The sight of her lying there, knowing that her life was tragically cut short so soon, is too much to bear.

"That's my sister; that's London," I mutter before bursting out into tears.

At Detective Andrews' desk, I try my best to remain composed. To calm my nerves, I take a sip of the earl grey tea that he was nice enough to fix for me.

"Can you tell me a little about your sister?" he asks.

I exhale deeply, "What do you want to know?"

He responds, "When was the last time you talked to London?"

I scratch my head; the last few days have been quite traumatic to say the least. Things are a bit blurry, but I try my best to sift through my memory.

"Umm, about a week ago," I reply.

"Did she say anything that was strange or make you feel like she was in trouble?"

"No, not that I can remember."

*If she was, I don't think I even noticed.*

I can't tell him that; it's far too embarrassing.

"Would you say that you two were close?" Detective Andrews asks.

I become irritated, "Close? Of course. Different, yeah, but we were very close. We came into this world together."

It's a bond that only twins would understand. He wouldn't get it.

"I'm sorry, I know that this is hard. I'm just trying to gather any information that will get me closer to our perp," he explains, interrupting my thoughts.

I nod, "What did they do to her?"

"It appears that your sister was stabbed. There was a struggle. She didn't go down without a fight."

I run my fingers through my hair.

Andrews continues, "Did London have any enemies?"

His question catches me off guard. I mean, she didn't exactly have a lot of friends, but neither did I. We didn't feel like we needed any of that because it had always been us. I'll admit, London was no saint. In fact, she did things that I'd never imagine doing, but that didn't mean that she had enemies.

I sigh, "No. Why do you ask?"

He states, "Well, we can't seem to locate her cellphone. But nothing else appears to have been taken so we're having trouble establishing a motive."

"Ok," I say.

"I'm waiting for more details from the autopsy report," he explains.

I can't fight back my tears and breakdown once more. Andrews places a sympathetic hand on my shoulder and hands me a Kleenex tissue.

"Thank you," I sniff.

I lift up my sunglasses to dot my eyes.

Andrews notices my eye immediately, "Care to tell me what happened?"

I quickly remember my bruising and want to kick myself.

"A pile of shoeboxes fell from my shelf and caught me in the eye," I lie.

He sits back in his seat; he doesn't seem to buy my story.

"What else do you want to know?" I ask, changing the subject.

"Was she dating anyone?"

"My sister dated, but commitment wasn't really her thing," I finally reveal.

"Do you know anyone that would want to hurt her?"

I quickly shake my head, "No."

"Ok, well, that's all I have for now. If you think of anything, anything at all, please give me a call," Detective Andrews says before handing me his business card.

I take it and place his information into my purse, "Will do."

I rise out of my chair, and he follows suit.

"Trust me, I'm going to do everything in my power to find the person that did this. You have my word," he promises.

"Thank you," I reply.

I walk out of there more confused than ever. My sister is dead, and someone made damn sure of that. I just can't figure out why. London wasn't the type of person to be reckless, but I have this burning feeling that she'd bitten off more than she could chew this time.

*What have you gotten yourself into, London?*

~

*Saturday, January 18, 2003*

I toss in my twin-sized bed, suddenly awakened by a loud noise. My eyes scan the room in a sleepy haze, but nothing is there. Annoyed, I try my best to fall back asleep, but then I hear it again. This time, I sit up in my bed and lean forward, trying to confirm what I thought I'd just heard. Moments later, I hear it once more, my sister's cries. I check my bedside clock. It's midnight. My mother wouldn't be home for another hour or so from her shift at the hospital.

Just then, I hear his voice, followed by a door shutting. I walk up to my door, carefully taking a peek into the hallway. As I do, I see Terrance, my mom's new boyfriend, creep back into her bedroom.

My heart races. Something is wrong. I can feel it. I take a deep breath and tip-toe across the hall to London's room. Once I open her door, I see her curled up in her bed, crying. Without saying a word, I'm at her side. She keeps her back facing me, but I can feel her body relax a bit when she realizes that it's me.

Over the last few months, Terrance has taken an inappropriate interest in my sister. I've noticed that he stares at her much longer than he should. He's always been overly eager to be nice to her, getting her candy and giving her money.

One day after school, she broke down, telling me everything. It started with him watching her, then touching. At first, it was him that was doing all the work, then one day he made her return the favor. She refuses to tell anyone, mainly because she is scared that no one will believe her. And that if she did, Terrance would kill her. Tonight, I have the dreadful suspicion that he took things to the next level. The realization breaks my heart.

"Did he hurt you?" I whisper.

London slowly nods, I can feel her body shiver.

I cry, disgusted, enraged and worst of all, powerless.

"Lon, you have to tell someone!" I plead.

"Shh! You'll wake him," she orders. "You promised you wouldn't say anything, Liv; swear to me," she cries, holding up her pinky.

I loop my pinky finger with hers, swearing to my twin, "I promise."

~

Memories of that night still sting my heart. I know that it changed my sister forever. Her innocence, her childhood was completely robbed from her. Now here we are, over seventeen years later, and her life has been robbed from her. Leaving my sister's side was one of the worst things I could've ever done. Dead or alive, I can't leave her side again.

*I won't let you down this time, London. I'm going to stay and see this through for you.*

*Whoever did this to you won't get away with this; they can't get away with hurting you, not this time.*

# LONDON

*Saturday, October 18, 2014*

"God, my life sucks right now!" I whine, as I dramatically flop down onto the large sectional couch.

"London, your life doesn't suck. You're just going through a rough patch; we've all been there," Inez, says.

I glance over at her with a half-smile. She's obviously trying to cheer me up, but I can't stop myself from swimming in my own pool of misery. In a matter of weeks, I've managed to get dumped, lose my apartment and get fired from my job. Although I appreciate her efforts, Inez isn't capable of understanding my struggles, not even a little bit.

I take a moment to admire her decked out one-bedroom apartment, designer handbags, and shoes, plus the brand-new Lexus that she has parked out front. In contrast, my life couldn't be more different. Here I am, crashing on my sister's couch and struggling to keep up with my bills.

*Shit, if I was living like this, I'd have an unwavering optimistic outlook on life too.*

I snort, "That's easy for you to say. You're practically rich!"

Inez laughs, clearly amused by my assumption, "I'm definitely not rich. Comfortable yes, but it comes at a cost."

"Oh? And what's that? Overbearing parents?" I tease.

Inez and I have only been hanging out for the last few months, but even though our friendship is relatively new, we've become surprisingly close. Normally, I kept to myself and didn't make many friends. But I remember the night we met like it was yesterday. It was my first shift waitressing at the Cocktail Club, and it was one of the worst days of my life. Try spending hours serving drunk, overly friendly, creepy men all while wearing super uncomfortable heels. To top it off, I had a table of men celebrating a bachelor party, and the groom greeted me by vomiting all over my chest.

Naturally, I locked myself in the bathroom, embarrassed and disgusted, not only with my new job but also myself. I guess Inez took pity on me because she helped clean me up and offered to take me out for a drink so that I could forget the whole ordeal. I have to say, one of my worst nights turned into the best night of my life thanks to her. Although she's nearly five years older than me, Inez is one of the most fascinating people I've ever encountered.

"Girl please, I haven't talked to them in years. I just happen to have generous friends," she explains.

"Friends? As in plural?" I quiz her.

Now that I think of it, I've never heard the girl talk about her family, work, or anything other than having a good time.

*How in the hell does she afford this luxurious ass life?*

I roll my eyes, "What, do you have a sugar daddy?"

I giggle to myself, clearly tickled by my own joke.

"Something like that," she says.

I nearly choke when I realize that she isn't joking; in fact, Inez is deadly serious.

Inez sits up, meeting my gaze, "Some men are willing to pay big bucks to be able to have women like us on their arms."

"Do you have sex with them?" I ask.

"Sometimes, but most of the time they just want a girlfriend for the night, a companion," she says.

I can't believe my ears, "That doesn't make you feel...dirty?"

She chuckles, "Dirty? No. Actually, it can be pretty fun. I've been on yachts, private jets, and halfway around the world."

I mean, it sounds tempting, but I'm still apprehensive at the whole idea of it.

"But aren't they using you? You don't feel taken advantage of?" I pry.

Inez's demeanor quickly changes from that of amused to solemn.

She looks me square in the eyes, "London, I made over five thousand dollars last week, just to go on three dates. Who is the one being taken advantage of?"

I nervously break our eye contact and look to the floor.

"What's dumb is being broken-hearted with nothing to show for it," she continues.

I sit back, stunned, and if I'm being honest, intrigued. She has a point.

Inez gently places her hand on mine, "I know that we just started hanging out, but I like you, London, and I want to help you. I'm telling you, if you let those inhibitions go and stop letting society tell you what to do with your body, shit, you can be out here getting paid just like me."

I sit back, pondering what she said. I mean, she brings up a good point. I've gone on plenty of horrible dates for free and have nothing to show for it.

*What's so wrong with getting paid for dating?*

Later that night, I'm unbearably anxious. The elevator walls seem to be closing in, and I can feel small beads of sweat forming across the back of my neck. I look to my right at Inez, who is as calm as the night sky. I self-consciously adjust my white midi dress for the tenth time. It feels like my heart is beating uncomfortably fast, so much that I swear that I can hear it over the elevator music. Moments later, a soft bell rings out above us, an indication that we've reached our floor.

"You look amazing, London. Remember to just keep calm and be nice; they won't bite," Inez says as we step off the elevator.

When we enter the lounge, a member's only spot that is frequented by the city's most wealthy. I look around, admiring the modern art, elegant platinum chandeliers and velvet couches.

"Reservation under Clark," Inez says to the attractive young hostess that welcomes us.

She smiles and leads us to our table. As we approach, I see two gentlemen sitting down having what looks like a deep conversation. Once they see us, they abruptly stop and stand to greet us. I'm shocked to see that they're both extremely attractive. Both donning expensive suits, well-groomed, and definitely enamored with what they see.

"Call me Mercedes," Inez whispers.

*Huh?*

Inez or, should I say Mercedes, is super affectionate as she hugs the first gentleman, "Leo! Hello, darling."

He's obviously the older of the two, I presume in his late forties or early fifties, given away by the sprinkle of gray hairs in his goatee. The two share a brief kiss before pulling away. I can feel his friend's eyes on me, but I'm too nervous to engage.

Leo wraps his arm around Inez's waist, "Ladies, I'd like for you to meet Mike, my business partner. Mike is from Baltimore and in town for the evening."

I finally look up, locking eyes with him.

*I can do this.*

*He's only in town for the night, and I'll never see this man again.*

I silently coach myself and try to calm my nerves.

Mike smiles and extends his hand towards Inez and then to me, "It's a pleasure to meet you both, Mercedes and?"

I lightly swallow, before taking his hand, "Porsha."

~

*Friday, March 1, 2019*

The soulful voice of Ari Lennox fills my apartment, and I mindlessly hum along to the lyrics. I step out of the shower and reach for my towel to dry off my body.

I'll be the first to admit, sleeping with men for money was never the plan. Honestly, I don't even consider myself to be an escort. I like to think of what I do as an experience; a service of emotion is what I like to call it. I help others, specifically men, forget their problems for a night while having their emotional, physical, and psychological needs met. I don't see any harm in getting paid for stroking a rich man's ego and looking good on his arm while doing so. In my opinion, they need me just as much as I need them, and there's nothing wrong with adding a simple business transaction to the mix to seal the deal.

Hell, just last month, I made nearly twenty thousand dollars. Where else can I make that type of money?

After moisturizing my skin and sliding into my black lace lingerie set, I take a seat in front of my vanity. My skin radiates as I brush on my favorite foundation, followed by a subtle coral blush. I carefully line my full lips with blood-red lip liner before filling them in with the same color lipstick. My phone rings as I put on my mascara. I reach over to retrieve it and see Inez's name across my screen.

Although I'm not ashamed of the lifestyle I choose to live, not many people know about it, not even my sister, Olivia. They just wouldn't understand. I'd rather not face the constant worry or questions that I know the people in my life would ask, especially Liv. She just wouldn't get it, and I don't want to trouble her. She's always been very protective of me, and I, her.

"Hey girl, what's up?" I answer.

"I catch you at a bad time, hoe?" she asks.

I giggle, "I'm getting ready to have dinner with Richard."

"His old ass," she jokes.

We both burst out laughing.

"You want to meet up after?" I ask.

"Maybe, I have a date with this new guy I've been talking to," she reveals.

"Oh? What happened to Quentin?" I ask.

"Girl! His wife found out and shut that shit down. Sent me a nasty email and paid me to leave her husband alone," she says.

I gasp, "What? How much?"

"Fifteen thousand dollars!"

"Did you take it?" I ask.

"Are you crazy? Of course, I did! But now I need someone to fill that gap; he was the one paying my mortgage," Inez says.

I shake my head with another chuckle, "See, I told you about messing with those married men. They're nothing but trouble."

I'm speaking from experience here. That's why I only deal with men that are either widowed, divorced or completely uninterested in commitment to anyone other than themselves now.

"I mean, they're not all bad," she argues.

After putting the final touches on my hair, I walk over to my closet and look through my wardrobe.

"Well I should be done around midnight tonight," I say, changing the subject. I was in no mood to argue about the moral code in our line of work. "Want to meet at our usual spot?"

"Of course. I'll see you later."

"Be safe, and don't forget to send me the drop pin of your location," I say as I settle on my dress for the night, a simple and sexy Gucci dress.

"Ok, mom, I will. Love you," Inez says with a laugh.

"Love you too," I reply as I slip on my dress and hang up.

Twenty minutes later, I hop into my midnight black CLS Mercedes Benz. I pull into Savona, an upscale Italian restaurant on the outskirts of town, and park in the empty spot next to Richard's royal blue Tesla. Once I put my car into park, he's on the driver's side, helping me out of the car.

"How's my favorite girl?" he smiles.

"I'm good," I say, greeting him before leaning in and giving him a kiss on his pale cheek.

"You look beautiful as always," Richard says.

"Thank you."

Richard is over twenty years my senior, with plenty of money to burn. You know the type that spend their mornings golfing and weekends at social clubs? In the three years since we've met, I've been on his private jet and skiing at his house in Aspen.

In reality, Richard is nothing but a lonely man that has commitment issues. According to him, his wife, the love of his life, died nearly five years ago from breast cancer. When we found one another, it was like the stars aligned; we both needed each other. I was getting over a dark time in my life, and he was heartbroken and lonely. We take care of each other. Not in a romantic lovers type of way, more so with our companionship.

We walk, hand in hand, into the restaurant and at Richard's request, get a seat outside on the heated patio. The hostess is noticeably surprised at our age difference. But the looks we get never bother us; we are used to the stares. After all, he is an older Caucasian man with a younger, beautiful, black goddess on his arm. It's not a pairing that you see every day. I can only guess the things that these people assume, but I don't give a shit. People and their thoughts of me had nothing to do with me paying my bills.

Normally, we get together once or twice a week. As I said before, Richard desires companionship, someone to enjoy lunch with, engage in small talk, and cuddling is usually all he wants. We've only had sex a handful of times during our entire relationship. Whenever we do, it's never anything to brag about. Don't get me wrong, Richard is still very handsome for his age, and I'm attracted to him, but he usually climaxes in less than five minutes. Honestly, I'm impressed that he can manage to still get it up.

Although sex is not a big part of our arrangement. Richard loves seeing me naked and especially enjoys watching me shower or bathe. Everyone has their fetishes, right? So, every so often, I'll strip down and let him watch me take a bath or shower. Whatever the request, he usually leaves very happy and gives me a bonus for my eagerness to meet his needs.

~

Back at Richard's place, he helps me out of the car and guides me inside his house. We make our way into his study, and I have a seat on the couch before taking my heels off and crossing my legs.

Richard heads over to his bar, fixing our drinks, two old-fashions. Once he's done, he joins me on the seat.

"How's work going?" I ask.

"Hectic, we've got a new client that is painstakingly needy. I've had to fly out to Seattle more times than I would like to," he explains.

One thing that I know about Richard, he loves when I take the time to actually ask him how he's doing and when I show interest in his work. Being the CEO of a software development company requires a lot of work, and it's easy to forget that he's human. At the end of the day, all he wants to feel is that someone gives a damn. That's where I come in and help. I provide emotional service, remember?

After twenty or so minutes of talking, he lets his hand stroke the exposed part of my inner thigh, "Are you ready for your bath?"

I take a sip of my drink and nod. Richard grasps my hand before leading me upstairs into his master bedroom.

"Wait here. I'm going to get everything ready," he instructs.

I nod again and take another sip of my cocktail. I hear him turn on the water and can see him lighting some candles, setting the mood. The smell of lavender and vanilla creep out of the bathroom. Moments later he returns, taking my hand and leading me towards my bath. My eyes light up when I see red rose petals floating in the bubble-filled tub.

"Aw, you're so romantic," I blush.

Richard softly kisses my hand, "Only for you."

Smiling, I finish off my old-fashioned before turning my back toward him, "Can you help me?"

He eagerly obliges, unzipping my dress and helping me step out of it. Without a word, I slowly unhook my bra before letting it drop to the floor. Mesmerized, Richard takes his drink and sits down, watching my every move. I slip my panties off and step into the tub. My skin instantly welcomes the warmth of the water as I sink in.

"Wash yourself," he commands.

I do as I'm told, reaching for the white loofa and bottle of Hermès Eau D'orange Verte shower gel strategically placed by my side. I gently squeeze the contents of the bottle out onto the loofa before rubbing it in between my hands. I use it to cleanse my body, starting with my neck and trailing to my breasts.

My hands gently caress my chest as the water rinses off the soap. I look over my shoulder and see Richard giving me his undivided attention. I can see the bulge forming in his pants, and it's not long before he finishes his drink off and begins touching himself.

Licking my lips, I continue to simultaneously wash and fondle myself, lifting one leg towards the ceiling so that he can see and gently scrubbing. It's not long before I let my hands explore my most private parts. I close my eyes and softly moan at the feel of my fingers rubbing against my pussy.

I can hear Richard's breathing grow heavy.

"You going to cum for me, baby?" I say.

That was enough to set him over the edge. He moans loudly, and I finish myself off as well.

After an hour or so of cuddling and kissing, Richard is fast asleep. I carefully remove his arm from around my waist and re-dress myself. I feel Richard stir beside me, and I give him a kiss on the lips.

"I have to go, love," I whisper.

He slightly grins before getting out of bed and walking into his closet.

"When are you free next week?" he calls out.

"Umm, I'm pretty much available all week except for Thursday and Sunday."

Richard reappears from the closet with a black envelope in his hand, "I have a few meetings out of town, but I'll call you when I return."

He reaches out his hand, giving me my money.

I smile, before taking it and leaning into him, "I'll be here waiting."

We share a tender kiss.

He smiles, "Thank you for tonight."

"Of course," I wink.

After sharing another kiss, I make my way out of his house and into my car, driving off into the night.

# OLIVIA

My mind races; the last two days have been a monsoon storm of raw emotion. I can't seem to catch my breath. Since leaving the police station, I've been cooped up in my hotel room, feeling devastated, helpless and unsure of what to do.

So, I order room service and hide from the world and my problems. Sometimes I cry; sometimes I sleep; sometimes I stare at the wall and contemplate smashing my head into it. I close my eyes as the water runs down my face and my body. The steam from the shower helps to calm my nerves a bit, but not much. There are so many questions and so few answers.

I've never experienced a loss like this. It feels like I've lost a part of my entire being. I can't think or even see straight. I'm completely lost. It's always been me and my sister, especially since our mother went away. I feel a sharp pain in my side as soon as the thought of our mother crosses my mind. I'm dreading having to break the news to her. She's been through so much. I know that this will break her heart.

The sight of London's lifeless body continues to haunt me. I can't shake the feeling that I let her down by not being here to protect or help her.

*How could she have been in trouble and not tell me?*

*How could I not even notice that she was in danger?*

*Marcus.*

I realize now that I was consumed by my tumultuous relationship with him. I wasn't always like this, and now I regret being so weak. I yearn to be the fearless girl I used to be, long before falling for Marcus. I feverishly scrub my skull, trying to erase his memory from my mind. A few minutes later, I step out of the shower and dry off. In the bedroom, I take a seat on the bed and power on the television.

When my mind isn't fixated on Lon, I'm panicking about how I should handle this Marcus situation. I've been back and forth about telling someone, anyone, about what I've done. The secret and the guilt are starting to eat away at me. I wonder if anyone has discovered his body yet, and how much time I have before the cops come looking for me. I'm half-expecting my photo to pop up onto the news channels or *America's Most Wanted* at any moment.

As I reach for the lotion and slowly rub it into my skin, I hear it.

"Breaking news tonight. A thirty-year-old woman was brutally murdered in her bed in Philadelphia. Police say they have no leads," the news reporter says.

I look up at the television screen and see a photo of London.

Once again, I break down and cry.

~

The winter cold is brutal and unforgiving. I stroll down the city blocks in Center City. The sidewalks are filled with pedestrians, and the streets are filled with cars, everyone eager to get to their next destination.

I enter South Jazz Club and see her sitting at the bar. I can't remember the last time that I had a drink or even a girl's talk. I feel bad because, since moving to Charlotte, I've been very distant from everyone. Once the news broke of London's murder, Avery called me and was eager to offer her support. She was relieved to hear that I was in town and insisted that we get together.

The moment Avery sees me, she gets up from her chair and pulls me into her arms, consoling me.

"I'm so sorry, Liv," she cries.

We stand there, hugging for a long while. It feels good to be hugged this way.

"How are you holding up?" she asks once we finally pull apart.

I shrug, "I don't know. It still feels like a bad dream."

She hugs me again, "You just take all the time you need. I'm here for you; just say the word."

I nod, fighting back tears, "Thank you so much."

We take our seats by the bar, and I really get a good look at my old college buddy. Avery is absolutely stunning. Her chocolate brown skin is silky smooth. She's sporting her signature pixie cut, a look that showcases her prominent cheekbones and compliments her almond-shaped eyes. Shortly after we take our seats, a bartender approaches us.

"What can I get you miss?" he asks.

"Can I get a martini please?" I say.

He smiles, "Coming right up." He turns to Avery, "And another martini for you?"

She nods and then turns to me, "Did you come back with Marcus?"

I quickly shake my head no, "I came alone. We broke up."

I figured I'd let it be known now before she asked any more questions.

She nods with complete understanding. I am sure I look so pathetic to her right now.

"Damn, I'm so sorry, Liv. Are you going to stay in Philly?" she asks.

I hadn't really given it much thought. But the truth is, nothing is left in Charlotte for me, and Philly is home, although there isn't really anything here for me either.

"For now, yes."

Luckily, the bartender returns and places our drinks down in front of us, interrupting my thoughts for a moment. I pick up my drink and take a sip, lightly tapping the cool glass on the side of my temple.

I turn to her, "How are you doing?"

"I can't complain," she says.

We spend time catching up and order another round of drinks.

"What about your business? The last time I saw you, you were getting booked left and right," I mention.

The mere mention of her event planning business brings a smile to her face.

"It's great, honestly; it's never been better. I doubled what I made last year already! I'm going to need to hire an assistant soon," Avery explains.

"That's amazing, Avery. I'm so proud of you, girl," I say.

Every word I said is true, but I'm also a little jealous. Listening to her talk about her life and all the amazing things that she has going for herself makes me realize how alarmingly different my life is. No family, no place to live, no job, a degree that I'm still paying for and barely any sanity. I'd give anything to spend a day walking in Avery's shoes, to have something to call my own, to have peace.

"Thank you, that means a lot, Liv," she says.

Halfway through my second drink, I turn to Avery, "Did you ever see London around? Like with anyone strange?"

She looks uncomfortable with my question at first but finally nods. "Yeah, at a private event I was working for a client. She was with this older white man, which I thought was strange."

My eyebrows furrow, "What do you mean with?"

"Like together, they were very close. He had to be almost sixty years old," Avery explains.

"You're sure?"

"Positive."

I stay silent and take a long sip of my drink.

Avery is apologetic, "I'm sorry, I shouldn't have said anything."

I touch her hand, "Don't be, I appreciate you telling me. Maybe I didn't know my sister as well as I thought I did."

The guilt of her death and not knowing more about her life or who she was is beginning to settle in. Frustrated, I take another sip of my drink.

As I do, a man, accompanied by a pretty, young woman enters the bar. I watch them, mindlessly admiring the woman's stylish Burberry coat. Suddenly, the man lays his eyes on me, and his eyes nearly bulge out of their sockets. I instantly look away, avoiding eye contact.

Avery and I continue talking and catching up. It's a welcome distraction from the chaos in my life. She's so easy to talk to; it is one of the things I love about her. By our third round, a group of older men sits at the bar. They're visibly drunk and are horsing around with each other. One looks in my direction and makes a pathetic attempt at flirting with me. I nervously scratch my head and finish off my drink much faster than I should have. Moments later, I start feeling dizzy and stand on my feet.

"I'll be right back," I announce.

She looks concerned, "You good?"

I nod, "Yeah, just need to use the restroom."

"Ok."

I make my way into the bathroom. Once there, I'm spiraling.

After splashing some water on my face and taking a few deep breaths, I dry off my hands. As soon as I open the bathroom door to exit and rejoin Avery at the bar, I nearly choke. The man that walked into the bar earlier with the woman is staring daggers at me. Before I can say a word, he takes my arms, powering his way into the restroom and roughly pushes me up against the bathroom stall. I try to scream, but he covers my mouth.

"You think I forgot about what you did to me bitch?!"

My heart races as confusion rushes over me.

"You and your friends stole over forty thousand dollars from me. I want my money," he sneers.

My eyes grow big.

"Forty thousand dollars? For what? I don't even know you," I cry.

"Don't play stupid, Porsha. I know that you and those girls set me up! I want my fucking money, or I will find you," he threatens.

Before I can protest, he glides out of the bathroom, leaving me struggling to catch my breath.

*Porsha?*

~

The next day, my nerves are on edge and my palms are sweaty. I take a deep breath before entering the police precinct. I'm anxious to see Detective Andrews. Being questioned by a homicide investigator is not something I want to do, especially not right now. But this is bigger than me and my sins. I'm willing to do anything that will help Andrews get closer to the killer.

When I walk in, he's waiting for me by the door.

"Thanks for coming in," he begins.

I nod and pull my leather gloves off.

"Follow me," he insists.

We walk in silence through the station, and I observe various detectives in their cubicles, hanging and chatting, some browsing the web. You'd think they'd find something better to do, like solve the tons of murders in this city, specifically my sister's.

Andrews can sense my annoyance, "Can I get you anything before we get started? Coffee, tea?"

"Water is fine," I reply.

He nods and leads me into an interrogation room. The walls are plain and white, and there's a single metal table in the middle of the room. I take a seat, and Andrews leaves me to my thoughts. Moments later, he returns with a bottle of water and a notepad in hand.

"Thank you," I say, as he hands me the water.

He carefully takes a seat in the chair directly facing me.

"You sounded really shaken up over the phone, is everything alright?" he asks.

"Yes, I'm ok, now."

Andrews looks concerned, "What happened?"

I reveal, "I was approached by someone last night. The moment he saw me, it was like he knew me, like I looked familiar. It really freaked me out."

"Then what?"

"He approached me while I was in the bathroom; he was really angry," my voice quivers.

"Did he hurt you?" he asks, and I can hear the concern in his voice.

I quickly shake my head, "No, not really. Scared the shit out of me is a better way to describe it. He grabbed me and pushed me against a wall."

"What did he look like; did you get a name?" Andrews asks, leaning forward in his seat.

I shake my head again, "It all happened so fast. I had a little too much to drink. You know, to get my mind off things. But he said that I owed him money, forty thousand dollars to be exact."

Andrews seems muddled, "And you're certain you've never met him before?"

"No, he called me Porsha," I say.

He leans back into his seat, confused, "Porsha? That's strange."

I nod, "Maybe it was just a case of mistaken identity."

"Or..." Andrews says as if he was pondering something.

"Or what?" I ask.

"He thought you were your sister."

# LONDON

*Tuesday, March 5, 2019*

So, how's boring ass Charlotte treating you?" I ask, clearly in an attempt to chastise my sister.

"Better than tired ass Philly," she counters.

I chuckle to myself before plopping down onto my mattress, "Whatever girl, Philly is home! You know you miss it."

There's no hesitation in her voice, "No, I miss you, that's about it. Philly isn't going anywhere."

I can sense her annoyance with my deliberate attempt to guilt her for moving so far away, but I can't help myself. We've never been this far apart from one another. Even though I'm trying my best to be happy for her and her relationship, I selfishly want to be closer to her.

Truth is, I've felt off ever since she revealed she was moving over three months ago. I can remember the day she told me; I instantly got this sinking feeling in my stomach. I mean, can you blame me? It's always been us, throughout the good and bad and downright ugly, through and through.

To make matters even more annoying, Marcus isn't someone I particularly care for. And I have no problem voicing my opinions to Liv, which I make sure to do quite often, but it is more than that. She has shrunken herself for this man; she's different. It's like she can't have a life outside of him. I guess she's in love and that's what some people do to show their commitment and devotion to their partners. Let's just say that is definitely not my style, not anymore. We're complete opposites when it comes to dealing with our male counterparts. But this is more than a difference in our dating styles; something isn't right. I can feel it. She's fading. Call it twin's intuition, but I know my sister.

If I'm being honest, Liv was a bit standoffish long before her move. There's no denying she's a moody person, and understandably so. She's been through a hell of a lot, and so have I. We definitely have different ways of dealing with our problems. When life gets to be too much, she often opts to shut down and keep to herself, while I prefer to be around the ones I love most.

A small part of me fears that she's hiding something. However, before I can allow myself to feel betrayed or get upset with her, I quickly remember that I've also neglected to be upfront and forthcoming about some of my own choices.

So, instead of being consumed by the lies and secrets we are obviously both keeping from each other, I decide to make the best of the time I do get with her and vow to be there for her when she's ready to come clean. I just hope that our secrets don't tear us apart.

"I miss you too, Liv; it's only been three months, and it feels like a year," my tone softens. "Did you get my housewarming gift?" I ask in an attempt to lighten the mood.

I can hear her smile through the phone, "Yes, I love them; thank you!"

"You better had," I joke. "Those things were expensive!"

We share a laugh and continue chatting for a few more minutes.

"How's the semester going?" Liv asks.

"Surprisingly, it's going really well. I have one last midterm to take before spring break begins, so I'm just going to study some," I explain.

"Nerd," she teases.

I roll my eyes, "Bye, girl."

"Ok, but tell me the fun stuff; any cute guys on campus?"

"Liv, what? I'm damn near thirty years old. I'm not worried about anyone on campus. They're practically babies," I argue.

"You're twenty-nine, relax," Liv says.

I laugh again, "That's thirty."

"What about the professors?" she pries.

"Well, there is my Psych teacher," I start.

Liv can't hold in her excitement, "Uh oh! What does he look like? Is he fine? How old is he?"

She shoots out her questions like a machine gun. I sigh and roll over onto my stomach, getting comfortable. Yes, Professor Harris is undoubtedly attractive. Sometimes it's hard to believe he is my teacher, but he is most definitely my type. He's tall, perfectly fit, and he has the most captivating, honey brown eyes. But Liv doesn't need to know all of those details.

"He's cute, but I'm not there for that. My main focus is making it to graduation," I say.

"Ok, well I'm proud of you, but that sounds pretty boring. You're supposed to be the exciting one," she teases.

"I'm sorry to be a disappointment," I rebuff.

Just then, I hear Marcus call out Liv's name in the background. He sounds upset.

"Lon, let me call you back," she instantly says.

"Ok, love you," I reply.

"Love you more," she says before hanging up.

I take a deep breath and resign to keep my thoughts to myself. Goodness, it's like I can't even have Liv to myself for ten minutes without him interfering.

"It's her relationship and her life," I tell myself.

After taking a few deep breaths, I return to my bedroom with a glass of water. Determined to ace my classes, I pull out my laptop and get back to studying.

~

*Tuesday July 4, 2017*

The soft kiss of the wind tickles my fingertips. I stretch my arms up to the night sky in pure bliss.

"Are you having fun over there?" he asks with a laugh.

I turn my attention over to him and sit back into the passenger seat of his convertible, "Are you going to finally tell me where we're going?" I ask.

Mike shakes his head, "It's a surprise."

"You said we would see the fireworks," I say.

"Be patient, love," he orders.

I hear his phone ring, and he quickly picks it up to look at it. Mike instantly becomes annoyed before typing a message and hitting send. My eyes fixate on his platinum wedding band for a moment. It must be his wife calling.

I sit back into my seat and watch the bright stars pass us by. Minutes later, I see a road sign for Annapolis, Maryland, and he takes the exit. My heartbeat quickens. I wonder what he has up his sleeve. I would've never imagined that being paid to be with someone would be so much fun. Mike was my first ever client, and I've grown to care about him so much. I wouldn't exactly call it love, but it's pretty damn close. Just then, we pull up to a boat dock. In the distance, I can see an array of yachts parked on the water.

"What's this?"

He ignores my question and gets out of the car before coming over to my side and helping me out.

"You don't want to miss the fireworks, do you?" Mike asks.

"What?"

"Come on," he says with a smile and takes my hand.

I can't hide my excitement as we approach a private yacht. I see the name Blue Moon painted across the stern. As we draw closer, I see a man holding a tray with champagne and a staff of people awaiting us.

Mike softly squeezes my hand, "How do you like my surprise?"

I smile, "I love it."

~

*Thursday, March 7, 2019*

*Beep!*

*Beep!*

*Beep!*

My eyes slowly open, and I stretch my arms out above my head. After a few moments of stretching and deep breaths, I reach over to my nightstand and grab my phone. It's nine-thirty in the morning.

When I see the time, my eyes nearly spring out of my head.

"Shit!" I exclaim before hopping out of my bed.

I had a late night with Richard, and I guess in my drunken and sleepy haze, set my alarm clock for nine-thirty instead of eight-thirty. My critical thinking exam is in less than an hour.

Panicked, I rush throughout my apartment. I brush my teeth and wash my face at warp speed. After pulling my blue jeans and oversized sweatshirt on, I tug my hair into a messy bun and stuff my laptop into my bag. My eyes quickly check my wall clock. If I leave now, I still have a shot at being on time.

Once I make sure that I have all of my essentials: cellphone, keys, books, laptop, and granola breakfast bar, I take a few deep breaths to calm my nerves. Spring break is only a few days away, and I can't wait for a week of solace.

Moments later, I rush out my front door and crash full force into another woman. The impact sends her falling to the floor, completely taken by surprise.

"Oh, my goodness! I'm so sorry, are you alright?" I say.

I'm by her side at once, helping to pull her up from the ground.

The woman is pretty, a little plain, but still pretty. She looks like she's around my age, but her eyes are strained, slightly tormented. I recognize the pain she's trying to hide immediately.

As I assist her, she forces a smile, "It's ok. Thank you."

"I'm such a klutz. I'm running a little late and apparently lost my ability to be aware of my surroundings," I explain.

She smiles again, a forced smile. I can tell that she's uncomfortable, shy even. Introverted, I get it.

"I've never seen you before; did you just move in?" I ask.

"Yes, just a few days ago. Apartment eight zero nine," she explains.

"Oh cool! I'm in apartment eight eleven. Welcome to the building. I'm London," I say, reaching out my hand.

Her eyes twitch slightly, but she takes my hand into hers, "Thank you, my name is Shay. It's nice to meet you."

I smile and look to check the time on my phone. Now I really have to get going.

"I'm sorry, I'm kind of in a rush. I'll see you around," I say.

My feet hurry towards the elevator and eagerly push the button. Moments later, when the elevator arrives, I step on and am shocked to see Shay still standing in the hallway. It looks like she's crying.

# OLIVIA

At my hotel, I'm still a bit shaken up by the other night and that scary bathroom encounter. Although it was extremely frightening, what Detective Andrews said shook me even more.

*Is he right?*

*Did that man mistake me for my sister?*

*If so, why was she telling people her name was Porsha?*

I step out of the shower and dry my body off. Once I finish, I reach for another towel and wrap it around my hair. I wipe the steam from the vanity mirror and stare at myself. I don't even recognize who I see anymore.

Suddenly, I hear a knock at my door and my heart jumps. I quickly grab the big white hotel robe hanging on the door and put it on, tying the long belt around my body. The knocks continue, and my heartbeat quickens. This is it, the cops tracked me down. I exhale before standing on my toes to look through the peephole. When I see that it's Detective Andrews, I relax a little.

After our last meeting, I gave him the information where I would be staying for a while just in case. During my interrogation, he got called to the scene of another murder, and he promised to resume our conversation. I wish that we could just forget the whole thing. He makes me nervous, and for some reason, I feel bad lying to him.

I take a deep breath and open the door. Once I do, he seems shocked at what he sees.

"Detective Andrews? Is something wrong?"

He looks agitated.

"Is this a bad time?" he asks.

I quickly shake my head no, "Come in."

I step aside as he enters my modest hotel suite. He looks around my room before turning to me.

"How are you holding up?"

I sigh, "I'm ok, I guess. Trying to get the funeral arrangements together."

He's sympathetic, "I understand. I'm glad to see that swelling has gone down."

My eye slightly tingles at his observation. I remain quiet for a moment, unsure of what to say.

"Do you have any more information on the case?" I finally ask.

He shakes his head, "I've checked into a few leads but no breaks in the case yet. Nothing substantial has come up; your sister seemed to have a lot of secrets."

"Tell me about it," I sigh.

I take a seat onto the bed and cross my legs.

"I know that you were very upset at our last meeting, and understandably so. Now that you've had a few days to process everything, do you have any information about your sister that will help the investigation? Anything at all?" he questions.

I contemplate his question for a second, trying to remember something, anything that will help him find the person that murdered London. Just then, I remember what Avery said.

"Apparently she was dating someone. He was nearly twice her age," I mention.

"Ok, this is good. Do you have a name?" Detective Andrews asks.

I shake my head, "No. But I thought that it was strange."

I remove the towel off of my head and lightly run my fingers through my hair. I look up and see him watching me, and I instantly become self-conscious.

"Umm, my friend saw her out with him at a party," I recount.

Andrews pulls out a small notepad and pen, scribbling something down.

"Do you have a description at all?"

"No, just that he was white," I reply.

He nods and continues to write.

I sigh, "I'm sorry. I wish that I had more."

"No, you're doing good. This is very helpful," Andrews smiles.

His phone rings, and he answers, "Andrews."

I watch him and can't help but to admire his prominent jawline; he's much more handsome than I remember. When he hangs up, he catches me staring, and I nervously look to the floor, tucking my wet hair behind my ear.

"I've got to run. Thank you for the information. I'll be sure to look into it," he reassures me.

Andrews can see the stress and my condition, "I'm going to try my best to find this perp."

I stand up, "Ok. Thank you for doing this."

I walk him to the door.

"It comes with the job, don't mention it."

I close the door behind him, pondering for a second.

*Who is this mystery man?*

*Did he kill her?*

~

The next day, I tap my foot and anxiously nibble away at my nails.

*I am in dire need of a manicure.*

The sound of the large metal door opening snaps me back into reality. I've been dreading this day since I arrived back in Philly.

My mother appears in front of me, accompanied by a stocky prison guard. She's stunned but visibly happy to see me. When I was younger, my grandmother used to drag London and I here just about every weekend, even though I begged to stay home. It's been a long while since I forced myself to come and visit her on my own; something London avidly disapproved of. She would come to see our mother every few weeks or so. I, on the other hand, haven't come to visit our mom in well over a year. I just hated seeing her like this.

I wait patiently as her shackles are removed, silently willing myself to keep my emotions together. Moments later, my chipper mother takes a seat directly in front of the thick glass window separating us. She looks good, considering the circumstances. Her hair is long and sprinkled with gray roots. Two long, braided pigtails hang aside both her ears, and her skin still looks as soft butter, just like I remember.

She smiles and quickly picks up the phone, "Hey, ladybug, it's so good to see you."

I try my best to put a smile on, "Hey, mama."

She quickly looks around, "Is Lon with you? I can't remember the last time you both came to see me at the same time."

The mention of London crushes me. I stare at my mother, the well of tears forming in my eyes.

"Mom," is all that I can manage to say.

Her once happy look quickly turns to worry, "What is it? What's the matter? Is it London?"

I try to speak but can't find my voice.

She reaches out and touches the glass, forcing me to look up at her. When I do, I can see she's desperate to understand what's going on.

"She's dead. Someone killed her," I finally say, crying.

My mother is frozen for a moment as if she can't believe the words she just heard. Suddenly, she belts out an agonizing cry. The other people in the visiting room start looking in our direction.

"Not London, not my London!" my mother sobs.

I can see her eyes searching for something, anything, to assure her that this is simply a horrible misunderstanding. But I have nothing. This is real, as much as I wish that it wasn't, it is.

"Olivia, please!" she screams, standing up suddenly, knocking her chair to the floor.

"Please, calm down," I beg.

But it's too late, the prison guard comes behind my mother in an effort to subdue her.

She yells, ignoring their orders, "You two were supposed to protect each other! What am I here for, huh? What am I here for if it was all for nothing?"

Her words hit me like a million daggers.

"I'm sorry," I cry.

I watch as my mother is dragged out and back to her cell.

Outside of the prison, I rush to my car. The sight of my mother and her breaking down that way was everything I didn't want to see. I feel awful, powerless and most of all, guilty. Not only did I let my sister down, but I also let our mother down too. A woman that gave up her life to protect her daughters. I can remember the day that she made us promise to always be there for each other and protect one another.

Inside my car, I rest my head on the steering wheel. Although I am relieved that it is over, I feel horrible. I wish that I could've just given my mother a hug. My phone rings, and I see that Andrews is calling.

*Good, maybe he has an update about catching the killer.*

"Hello," I answer.

"I have news; are you busy?" he says.

I sniff, "Not really, what's going on?"

He sounds concerned, "Are you alright?"

"I don't know," I confess. "What's the news?"

"I just finished talking to the medical examiner; they gave me the autopsy report," he explains.

I instantly notice the discomfort in his voice.

"What is it? What's wrong?" I ask.

"Your sister was ten weeks pregnant."

# LONDON

*Saturday, March 29, 2003*

B*aby boy, you stay on my mind*
*Fulfill my fantasies*
*I think about you all the time*
*I see you in my dreams*

The Saturday morning sun shines brightly into my bedroom. I turn up my radio and continue to sing along to Beyoncé's newest single. I dutifully make my bed and then proceed to put my folded laundry away. Mom has been hounding me for the last few days to clean my room, and I am eager to get her off of my back.

Truth is, I started neglecting keeping my room clean on purpose. The pile of clothes in the corner, trash, and shoes scattered across the floor, and the dirty sheets were my desperate attempt at keeping Terrance away from me. I'm not normally this sloppy, and my mother and sister have definitely noticed. But deep down, I'd hoped that the mess would make Terrance rethink his desire to touch me. Sadly for me, I was wrong. He hasn't stopped sneaking into my room at night. And I'm afraid to admit that I don't think anything will.

An hour later, I'd just about wiped down and disinfected everything in my bedroom. I stand and stare at myself in my full-sized mirror hanging behind my door. My eyes carefully examine every inch of my adolescent body. My breasts seem to be bigger than they were yesterday, but it's more than that. I feel different. My hands softly trail over my stomach. I close my eyes and pray for a sign.

Mere seconds later, it's like God himself heard my prayer; my bedroom door swings open. My mother charges in with rage-filled eyes. I'm immediately alarmed; something is wrong. She's holding something in her hand. My panties. The panties that Terrance made me throw away because he ejaculated in them.

"You little fast-ass!" my mother accuses.

She starts to slap and hit me across my face.

"I thought I told you about hanging around those nasty ass boys, London!" she pulls my hair and throws me onto the ground.

"Mama, please!" I scream.

My cries go ignored.

"You're not going to be doing this in my home, do you hear me? So, help me God, you and your sister are going to make something of yourselves! If you get pregnant, I swear to God!" she yells.

Olivia rushes into the room, and she's at my side in an instant, protecting me from my mother's angry blows. That does little to stop her from pouncing on me yet again. With tears in her eyes, Liv looks at me, urging me to tell our mother the truth. I clamp my mouth shut and endure the pain. I'd rather be beaten a thousand times than utter those words. Olivia just doesn't understand the shame that comes with being raped by someone.

Moments later, my mother is exhausted.

Her chest heaves as she saunters back out of my bedroom, "Keep your ass in this room. You're both grounded!"

Thankfully, she leaves. Allowing Liv and I to cry in each other's arms.

~

*Saturday, April 27, 2019*

It's the perfect spring day. I step out of my apartment building and take a deep breath before smiling. Philadelphia in the spring is one of my favorite places to be during this time of year. The flowers are in bloom, the days are longer, and the city is in a better mood, especially after suffering through a long and unforgiving winter. After ensuring that my leather tote is secured across my shoulder, I make the short walk towards my neighborhood coffee shop. It's finals week, and my nerves are all over the place.

Just as I round the corner, my phone rings; it's Inez.

"Hey, boo," I say once I answer.

"Hola, chica! What's up; what are you doing?" she asks in a super chipper mood.

"Same ole,' same ole;' about to get some studying done," I say.

"On a Saturday! Come on, girl, I know you're all about getting your education, but don't you want to take advantage of this beautiful day and meet me out for some fun?"

"Sounds tempting, but I have to get this done," I explain.

"Ok," she says. "How about tonight? I got the ins on a party happening later. There's going to be some serious money there."

The moment she says that, I know exactly the type of party she is referring to. These parties amongst our circle have become legend. Secret location, invite-only, and the average girl walks away with nearly twenty thousand dollars each. I can't lie, I'm tempted, especially because I have to pay for my summer classes in a few weeks. This opportunity isn't something that comes along every day.

I can see the coffee shop in the distance and decide to cut our conversation short, "Ok, count me in."

"My girl! See you tonight," Inez says.

"Ciao," I say before hanging up.

I place my phone into my bag and enter the establishment. The walls are wooden and white; various baked goods are on display on a marble tabletop.

After approaching the counter, I'm greeted by a curly-haired barista, "Hi, welcome to Peddler Coffee, what can I get you?"

I smile, "Can I have a vanilla latte with almond milk, please?"

"Sure thing, anything else?"

I quickly scan over the menu but can't settle on anything. Suddenly, a man stands beside me, and it's a little too close for comfort. When I look up, I'm shocked to see Professor Harris.

He smiles and turns towards the barista, "I'll take an Americano. Anything else for you, London?"

"No, nothing else for me," I manage to say.

The barista punches the order into the store iPad, "That'll be six dollars and ninety-five cents."

Without hesitation, Professor Harris hands her a ten-dollar bill, "Keep the change."

We step aside, waiting for our coffee.

"You didn't have to do that," I say.

He shrugs, "It's not a big deal, really."

"Thank you," I say.

"My pleasure. What brings you here?" he asks.

"Well, I have this huge paper that I have to write. My psych professor is expecting a massive argumentative essay on social media and if it's beneficial or dangerous for modern society," I sarcastically explain.

We both laugh. Shortly after, the barista returns with our drinks.

"Thanks, Alyssa," he says to her before grabbing our order.

"Oh, do you come here often?" I ask as we make our way towards an open table and stools.

He nods, "I do. They have some of the best roast blends in the city if you ask me."

I take a seat and sip my latte. Almost instantly, I'm blown away by how great it tastes.

Professor Harris smiles and sits, "See, what did I tell you?"

"This is amazing," I answer.

"Now back to this essay, I'm certain that your professor, whoever he or she is, is looking forward to reading your point of view on the subject," he says.

For some reason, I become nervous.

*Is he flirting with me?*

I want to ask, but I'm sure that if I do, I'll only end up making a fool of myself. He's my teacher, for goodness sakes.

So, instead, I say, "I'll be sure to knock this one out of the park."

Just then, he places his free hand on my shoulder, "I know that you'll do great, London. You're extremely intelligent; trust and believe in that."

My heart flutters.

"I, umm. Thank you, Professor Harris," I manage to say.

"Chase," he winks.

*He is flirting with me!*

I nervously bite my lip and look to the floor, something I'd normally never do in front of or because of a man. But this is different. I'm excited, and it feels quite strange.

"I'm more than just a teacher, you know," he jokes.

I laugh, "I know, I know. What made you want to teach?"

He seems touched by my question, "Honestly, my father; he was one of the best men I've ever known. Back in the day, he used to teach history up at Central High School. He always taught me that a black man's greatest weapon is his mind; we've got to be twice as smart. According to him, a great education is the only way that we will overcome all the bullshit this country has put us through, and we have to lift each other up. I guess I am just doing my part, you know?"

"Wow, that's deep and very admirable," I say.

Chase smiles and checks his wristwatch, "Looks like I've got to get going. Enjoy the rest of your weekend and good luck. I really do look forward to reading your essay, you've been an absolute pleasure to teach."

"Thank you, Chase. I really appreciate that," I say.

"See, that wasn't so hard," he teases.

I laugh, embarrassed again.

"See you around," he says.

"Bye," I reply as I watch him leave.

Once he does, I can see the barista watching me with a smile on her face. My face flushes, and I immediately feel self-conscious. I quickly pull out my laptop, ignoring her. The only thing that I want to think about right now is this paper; it has to be perfect.

Later that night, I put the final touches on my hair. Just as I complete the last few curls, my cell goes off, and it's Inez.

"Hello?"

"Pulling up, you ready?" she asks.

I stare at my dolled up face in the mirror, "Yup, I'll be right down."

Minutes later, I hop into Inez's white Panamera Porsche. After sharing a quick hug, she pulls off into the traffic. We are en route to the party.

I lean back into my seat, watching the buildings pass by, "How did you manage to get in on this party?"

Inez quickly looks in my direction with a smile, "Ok, don't be mad. Stormy invited us."

The moment I hear the mention of Stormy, I roll my eyes. Inez knew to keep that minor detail under wraps when she told me about this party earlier today. If I had known that Stormy was going to be involved, I would've said no without any hesitation, yet here we are.

Stormy, as fun as she could be, is bad news. I try my best to stay as far away from that girl as I can. Unfortunately, she and Inez are really cool. So, every so often, Inez attempts to have us all go out together. I wouldn't say that I don't like Stormy, per se, in fact, she can be really nice. But that's the problem. I never know if she's pulling a fast one on me. She's a master manipulator and loves toying with people, especially men. Now I don't know all the details of all that she does, but I do know that she's made it her business to screw people over. By the time they realize what's happened to them, she's long gone and on to the next.

"She's really not that bad, London," Inez offers. "Plus, she thinks you're such a sweetheart."

I sigh, "I guess."

Ten minutes pass, and we exit the car, leaving it with the building's valet attendant. We enter The Logan Hotel and walk to the elevator.

"So, now that I know the truth, what kind of party is this exactly?" I ask Inez.

"Easy money," she says.

*Hmph, we'll see about that!*

Moments later, we reach the top floor and make our way towards the Presidential Suite. I can hear music playing on the other side of the door. Inez reaches out her hand, knocking three times.

Stormy opens the door, and she's beaming, "About time you ladies got here."

She looks amazing; that's easy because Stormy is abnormally beautiful, like supermodel beautiful. Her hair is jet black and bone straight, resting at the middle of her back. The Cherokee blood that runs through her veins is prevalent through her bronze-colored skin tone. Although she stands at about five foot nine without heels, she's rocking six-inch Christian Louboutin stilettos with a skin-tight red dress.

Inez is the first to give her a hug before walking inside. I follow her lead and give Stormy a hug as well. When we pull away, I check out the room. Initially, I'm impressed; it's very nice, and the view is spectacular. Then I notice there's only one other person in the room. He's seated on the couch, watching us.

"Adam, these are my friends, Mercedes and Porsha," Stormy says.

Adam finally rises from the couch and greets each of us, "Wow, Jada said that you all were gorgeous, and she wasn't lying. Thanks for coming."

"I told you, baby, only the best of the best," Stormy, or in this case, Jada, says.

"Now we can get this party started. Would you like some drinks, ladies? We have champagne," Adam says.

Inez and I nod, before taking a seat. Adam is just about to head to the bar, but Stormy stops him.

"You sit down, get to know the girls. I'll make the drinks," Stormy orders.

He obliges her and rejoins us, sitting between us on the couch. My eyes dart in both Inez's and Stormy's directions.

*What in the hell did these two get me into?*

*A fucking foursome?*

I get it, we get paid to have sex for a living. But I did not sign up for this. Seconds later, Stormy returns with our drinks, handing them to us. She disappears again, taking Adam's glass to give him a refill. Once everyone has their drinks, we toast to the night. Minutes and small talk go by, and Adam visibly gets comfortable, resting his arm over my shoulders and finishing off his champagne.

Then he turns to me, "I want you all to get undressed, but leave your heels on."

Before I can protest, Stormy lightly touches my arm, and whispers so low that I can barely hear her, "Trust me on this."

I swallow hard, rising up from the couch, followed by Inez and Stormy. One by one, we strip off our clothing, standing naked in nothing but our stilettos. Adam is pleased. He stands before us and unbuttons his shirt before taking it off and throwing it to the floor. Next, he moves to his pants, refusing to take his eyes off of us. He struggles with his belt buckle.

"Don't make us wait forever, baby," Stormy teases.

Just as he is about to say something, his eyes roll back into his head, and he falls back onto the couch, completely blacked out.

"Oh my God!" I scream.

I'm by his side at once, frantically feeling round to check for a pulse. Suddenly, I hear him snore loudly.

"Damn, that took forever!" Inez says.

I whip my head in her direction, "What the fuck are you talking about?"

"Easy money, remember? You didn't think we were actually going to fuck him, did you?" Inez says.

"Are you crazy? What if he dies?" I ask.

Stormy says, "He's not going to die. He's just going to be asleep for a few hours."

Flustered, I watch her as she goes into his suitcase, pulling out money. She's holding over forty thousand dollars in her hands.

I'm instantly pissed, "Are you fucking kidding me? You both were in on this the whole time?"

Inez can see that I'm fuming and puts her hands up, "I knew that you wouldn't agree to it if I told you the truth. Stormy needed a favor."

Before I can go in on her, Stormy is by my side, and she hands me twelve thousand dollars.

"Thanks for your help tonight; you were great."

I stare at her and then the money.

*What the fuck?*

# OLIVIA

*Tuesday, April 8, 2003*

I stare at the large wall clock, mindlessly counting the seconds that pass by. I'm up to two hundred and thirty-seven. It's amazing how time always seems to go by so slow when you're in a hurry.

*Tick.*

*Toc.*

*Tick.*

*Toc.*

I anxiously tap my foot. Mom would be expecting us to be back home soon. Since the huge blow-up with London, she's been keeping us on a tight leash. We have to come home right after school and aren't allowed to go anywhere on the weekends. I guess that, in her mind, she's protecting us. Little does she know the problem isn't our friends or the neighborhood boys. The danger is waiting for us at home and sharing her bed every night.

"Will you stop tapping? You're making me nervous," London says.

"Sorry," I offer.

She crosses her leg and fixates on the television, a re-run of the popular music video countdown show; 106 & Park, is on. As the latest B2K video plays on the screen, I can't seem to focus. It's risky even being here. London decided to skip school and come, even though I begged her to wait. But it's the only way.

I turn to her, "You're not scared?"

She sighs, "Yea, of course, I am. But I'd be even more scared if I kept it."

I ask, "Are you sure you want to do this?"

She nods, holding firm in her position, "I'm not having that disgusting motherfucker's baby. I'd rather die."

We weave our fingers together, holding each other's hand, and I rest my head on her shoulder. I hate this. I hate feeling powerless. I sat up every night this week contemplating telling our mom the truth. But I know that if I did, London would never forgive me for betraying her trust.

Moments later, a petite nurse opens the waiting room door and calls out, "London Burrows?"

We both stand and make our way over to her, still holding hands.

Just as I was going to walk back with them, the nurse stops me, "Only the patient is allowed in the room. You're going to have to wait out here."

"I'm not leaving my sister," I protest.

London turns to me, "I'll be ok, promise. I won't be too long."

We hug before she pulls away. I want to challenge her because I know that she's lying. She's scared shitless, and so am I. I nod and step aside as angry tears fill my eyes. I don't want to make this any more difficult than it already is. Instead, I'm left standing there watching them walk down the long empty corridor.

~

Soft, white snow blankets the earth. A single snowflake lands on my leather glove. I stare at it, watching it melt to nothing.

"Merciful father, as we mourn the death of London and thank you for her life, we ask that you look upon us with compassion. Draw near to us Lord, and may we find comfort and peace in your presence. Give rest to our troubled hearts and replace our fear with faith. Amen," the priest recites.

"Amen," the congregation says in unison.

As my sister's casket is lowered into the ground, I sit unmoving, numb. Despite the cold, I stay that way for a good while. One by one, distant family and friends depart, dropping white roses on top of her grave and offering me their prayers and condolences. I try my best to be polite, but I can't help but feel like a giant fish in a tiny fish bowl. Everyone is here to spectate, passing judgment on London and myself, yet again. Honestly, it irritates me.

As much as I go through each day wishing this was a bad dream, reality finally sets in. This is real. London, my sister, is gone forever. My tears come to the surface, and I can't keep it together.

Time passes, and the cemetery attendants approach. They start breaking down the chairs around me and filling her grave with the dirt. Suddenly, a woman approaches alongside me with tears in her eyes.

She sniffs, "You're her sister, Olivia, right?"

I nod.

"I'm sorry," she says.

"Who are you?"

"I'm Shay; your sister was my neighbor and friend," she says.

"Thank you for coming," I say.

I never heard London mention this woman before. But as I've come to terms with her death and the life she lived, it's become apparent that there was a side to her that I didn't know.

"I know that you don't know me, but your sister had a profound impact on my life," Shay explains.

I smile, touched. London tended to have that effect on people.

"That sounds like London," I sniff.

Shay looks to her feet, nervous.

"Thank you for coming, Shay, and it was nice to meet you. If you don't mind, I'd like to have a few moments to be alone," I say.

"I understand, take care. Once again, I'm very sorry for your loss. Maybe I'll see you around," Shay says.

I force a smile and watch Shay retreat in the distance. I stand and walk over to my sister's grave. I kick at the dirt, trying to find the right words.

"I'm so sorry, London. I'm so sorry that I wasn't there for you. But why did you keep so much of your life from me? We weren't supposed to have secrets, London," I vent. I take a moment to calm myself, "I guess I didn't make it easy, and I'm sorry. I promise you; I will find whoever did this to you. I swear on my life."

Ten minutes later, I finally make my way back to my car, determined to bring my sister's killer to justice. As I do, I see a man standing by the trees. He's tall, brooding and very handsome. I've never seen him before, but it's clear that he doesn't want to be seen. Just then, he sees me watching him and instantly becomes uncomfortable, suspicious even. He quickly turns on his heels, making it crystal clear that he shouldn't be here.

Against my better judgment, I follow him. My inner voice is screaming at me to stop, but I can't stop my feet from moving. I watch him as he jumps into his car, and I quickly get into mine. I start up my engine in a hurry, eager to track him down. Just as I put my foot on the gas, I hear a loud horn beep and another car coming to a screeching halt just inches from my car.

*Jesus, Olivia, get it together.*

~

*The snow falls from the sky, hitting my face. The coolness of the fluffy snowflakes is soothing. My skin is burning hot for some reason, and I'm struggling to catch my breath. I watch as the snow continues to fall and land onto the ground before me. It looks so white and pure, and as soft as the clouds above. Then, she appears, taking me by surprise.*

*London looks as beautiful as ever. Her skin is glowing and smooth.*

*"London!" I gasp.*

*In an instant, I'm hugging her, unwilling to let go. She softly strokes my hair, and I inhale deeply, taking in her sweet smell of jasmine. We pull away, and she looks deeply into my eyes.*

*"Run!" she orders, her voice echoes in the wind.*

*Before I can protest, she vanishes into thin air. I reach out to feel her, longing to touch her one last time, but she's gone. I can't stop the tears from coming. Suddenly, a drop of ruby red blood lands right at my feet. I quickly look around, trying to investigate the blood's source.*

*"Olivia!"*

*The sound of his voice instantly sends chills down my spine. Marcus is facing me. His chest rises and falls, heaving with fury. The rage in his eyes petrifies me. I instantly start running, and the bright drops of red blood continue to drip, leaving a trail on the white snow. Instinctively, I reach up, wiping the cold from my nose, but to my horror, when I pull back my hand, it's covered in blood.*

*My heartbeat quickens, and I can feel him closing in on me. Suddenly, his hand grips my arm. I try my best to fight him off, but he throws me onto the ground. Marcus uses his rough hands to turn me over onto my back. He's choking me. I stare into his blood-red eyes, and cry, pleading. I don't want to die. I can slowly feel the air leaving my lungs until I can no longer breathe.*

~

"Aargh!" I scream.

My body shivers in a cold sweat. I carefully look around my hotel room in a panic. I reach up to touch my neck. I can still feel his fingertips on my skin. Frantic, I pull myself out of bed and walk into the bathroom to splash water into my face. The uneasy feeling in my gut refuses to settle.

"It was only a dream," I tell myself.

# LONDON

*Friday, May 31, 2019*

I make my way into Rouge, the new and hottest hangout in the city. My eyes scan the crimson nightclub, in search of Inez. As I do, I carefully navigate through the crowd, warding off advances from eager, and clearly intoxicated men. Blame it on the color scheme, but I can sense everyone in this place is pretty hot and heavy.

Luckily, it doesn't take me too long to spot her, along with Stormy. I instantly become aggravated.

"It's about time you made it!" Inez teases with a hug.

Stormy leans in front of her, giving me two quick kisses on either side of my cheeks, "Hey, London."

"Hello, Stormy. I didn't know you were coming out," I say, cutting my eyes at Inez.

"Well luckily for you two hags, I'm here! What are you drinking?" she asks.

I look down at our table and see that they're drinking champagne, "Champagne is cool."

"Coming right up!" Inez says.

Just then, I realize that I have to use the restroom, to pee, yes, but also, I want to get my mood in check so that I won't be a complete bitch all night. I really am not in the mood to deal with Stormy and her unlimited bag of tricks tonight.

"I'll be right back," I say.

Before either of them can offer to join me, I turn and head straight for the bathroom. After I'm done handling my business, I slowly wash my hands and close my eyes to take a few deep breaths and calm my nerves.

"London? Is that you?" a soft voice says.

I open my eyes and am shocked to see Shay. She looks out of place in an establishment like this because she is. This girl is the epitome of cookie-cutter and squeaky clean from what I can tell. Since bulldozing her to the floor a few months ago, we've run into each other a few more times. From what I can gather, she's a nice woman, but she's a little strange. I could've sworn one day she was listening in on one of my conversations as I was walking down our hallway, but I can't be sure.

"Shay? Hey! What a surprise," I admit.

She nods, "I know, right? I never thought I'd be in a place like this."

"Neither did I. What's the occasion? Are you here with anyone?" I ask

"No, I'm still getting to know the city, decided to step out and came to this place," she explains.

"How do you like it? It's different from Maryland, I bet," I say.

She nods, "It's so different. I feel really out of my league, honestly."

"Don't. How about you kick it with me? I'm out with some friends," I offer.

"Really?"

I smile, "Yes, now you can say you're having a night out with the girls."

She looks down at her drink, "Honestly, I don't know if I can keep up with you all. I think I've had too much to drink. Do you want this?"

I take the glass of champagne, "Sure, no sense in letting a drink go to waste."

I quickly throw it back.

Minutes later, Shay and I rejoin Inez and Stormy. Unsurprisingly, they're not alone.

"Wayne, Kyle, and Andres, this is my friend, London," Inez says, making my introduction.

The fellas rise up from the velvet red couch, visibly pleased to have two more beautiful women in their company. I'll admit, the trio is definitely nice on the eyes. The darkest of the three, Wayne, could give Kofi Siriboe a serious run for his money. No lie, the man was fine! His skin illuminated a midnight black, complimented by a Caesar low haircut and tapered beard. While his friend, Kyle, standing to his right is equally as handsome. In contrast, I can see the natural golden-brown highlights in his hair, a little curly on top and taken in on the sides. This one has a honey complexion and light hazel eyes. The third, Andres, is sexy and mysterious. He's Latino with a latte skin tone, tall and has phenomenal bone structure, complemented by full, pillowy lips. We lock eyes for a moment, and I lick my lips. I can feel Shay sway beside me.

"Everyone, this is Shay, my neighbor," I explain.

They all greet her, but I can tell Inez and Stormy aren't too thrilled with her joining us. After all, she is an accessory to our little party, but I don't care. I ignore them and pull Shay with me to take a seat onto the couch.

Inez hands me my drink.

Once I sit down beside her, she leans into my ear and whispers, "Andres is yours."

"So, Shay, do you drink?" Stormy asks.

Shay smiles, "Not really, but I'll have one."

"I thought you had too much to drink?" I ask.

She shrugs, "I think that I can handle one more."

Stormy grabs an empty glass and pours her drink before passing it to her. Shay nervously takes a sip and tries her best to blend in.

"Viva la Vida!" Stormy says, with her glass held high.

I take a long sip and get comfortable and socialize amongst our group. Minutes later, the DJ puts on the old-school and popular reggae record "Murder She Wrote," and Inez hops up.

"Oh, this is my song! Come on," Inez says, pulling Wayne up off the couch.

I chuckle to myself before finishing my drink.

Then, I see Andres with his hand out, "Want to dance?"

"Sure," I say.

I take his hand, standing to join him beside Inez and Wayne. Stormy stays behind on the seat, giving Kyle her complete attention, leaving Shay all alone. She watches us, leaning back and sipping her drink.

Inez throws her arm around Wayne's neck and slowly winds her hips to the music; the two are completely into one another. Andres and I start dancing, and I roll to the beat, matching his rhythm. I don't know if it was the song or all of the champagne I had, but I really start to let loose. I can feel his hands move to my hips and ass but don't stop him. Instead, I close my eyes and get lost in the music for a moment.

Suddenly, I feel strange. It's like my body is floating above the room. The music seems louder. I can feel it pulsating in my ears. My heart is racing, and my skin tingles from the sensation of Andres' hands on the small of my back. Then, without warning, everything goes black.

The next morning, I slowly open my eyes as the late morning sun creeps through my sheer white curtains, brightening the room. After a moment of adjusting my focus, I sit up in my bed and slightly stretch my arms up to the ceiling. I look down and see that my dress is still on. I rub my forehead, trying to remember when and how I got home. Suddenly, my front door opens and closes.

*What the hell?*

"Hello? Who's there?" I call out.

Moments later, my bedroom door opens, and Shay walks in holding bagels, Tylenol and Pedialyte.

"Good morning," she smiles.

"Morning," I say, confused.

She approaches the bed, "Glad to see you're doing better."

"What happened last night?" I ask.

Shay takes a seat on the foot of my bed, "We were all out, me, you and your friends, Inez and Stormy. You were dancing with some guy and then you kind of fainted."

*Holy shit!*

"Oh my God, are you serious?" I say, completely embarrassed.

Shay nods, "Yes, I managed to drive you home and get you into bed. I only kept your key so that I could check on you."

She sets my keys down onto my nightstand. I'm shocked by her kindness. Who knows what would've happened if she hadn't been there.

"Wow, Shay. I don't know what to say. I'm mortified right now," I admit.

She smiles, "Don't be. I'm just happy to see that you're doing ok."

"Thank you for helping me," I say.

"You're welcome," she pauses. "I have to ask about those women you were with last night. Are you sure they're your friends?"

"Huh? Why do you ask?" I say with caution.

I get that she helped me, but she is crossing a line.

"Well, I heard Stormy say she might've given you too much. I think that they slipped something into your drink," Shay says.

I can't believe my ears. But as I slowly piece the night before together, it starts to make sense. Drugging was Stormy's specialty, and I stupidly allowed them to make my drink. The reality hits me like a ton of bricks.

"Those fucking bitches," I say.

~

*Wednesday, June 5, 2019*

The city lights illuminate the night sky, and the soft spring breeze tickles my skin as I hop out of my Uber. I pull out my compact mirror and quickly check my makeup. Once I'm pleased with my appearance, I make my way inside Louie Louie, a charming, French-inspired restaurant nestled in University City.

Once inside, I'm greeted by a handsome host, "Good evening, table for one?"

I shake my head, "Reservation for Young."

He promptly nods and leads me to my table. Moments later, I see my date tapping his foot and scanning the menu. He looks nervous; nervous is good. I can usually swoop in and take control from the beginning of the date. If I had to guess, I'd say it was his first time; he wants to be told what to do.

Luckily, he is a lot cuter than I expected. When it comes to dealing with these fellas, it's really the luck of the draw as far as physical attraction goes. It's never stopped me from closing the deal, but it makes things easier when I'm truly attracted to them.

Once he sees me, his eyes widen. I guess that's a sign that he appreciates my gold satin dress, which hugs all of my curves and leaves very little to the imagination.

The host leaves us, "Your waitress will be right with you."

Don stands to his feet, "Porsha?" he confirms.

I smile and nod, "It's so nice to finally meet you."

I lean into him, giving a small kiss on the cheek. He helps me slide into the booth before joining me, getting very close to me, a little too close. I play it cool and look through the menu. We order our drinks and get acquainted. It only takes our waitress a few moments to return with our orders.

"You're absolutely gorgeous," Don compliments.

"Thank you," I say, before taking a sip of my champagne.

He asks, "How old are you?"

"Didn't you ever hear that it's rude to ask a woman her age?" I say, annoyed.

He giggles, "I mean, you don't look a day over eighteen."

I roll my eyes, "Here's hoping."

Twenty minutes and our second round of drinks later, we're greeted by our waitress once more, "Would you like another round?"

"Yes, and the check," Don says.

Moments later, she returns with our drinks, and I quickly take a sip.

Don finishes his off and leans into my neck, "I can't wait to get you upstairs."

He puts his hand on my thigh and slowly strokes it under the table. My heart sinks; something about this guy is beginning to creep me out. For some reason, Terrance pops into my head. I can remember the smell of whiskey on his breath and how every time he touched me, he made my skin crawl. The memory makes me want to vomit. I keep my cool and gently put his hand back to my knee. What's with these guys that think just because they've paid for a certain experience, that we have absolutely no class or morals?

"Come on, baby, you're so sexy. You've got me so hard right now," he pleads.

This time his hand trails up to my breast and slightly squeezes.

"Don, not here," I say, pushing his hand away.

"I'm not paying you five hundred dollars an hour to sit here and talk all night," he hisses.

He takes my hand, trying to pull it towards his penis.

"What the hell are you doing? Stop it," I order.

The last thing I want to do is cause a scene. He's obviously drunk, but he's crossing a major line.

He puts his hand over my mouth, "Shut the fuck up, bitch."

Now I feel myself panicking. My eyes scan the room, hoping that someone will notice. My heart nearly stops when I see Chase rushing over.

"Aye man, let her go," he orders Don.

Fists balled, Chase is furious. Don, who still grips my wrist, completely ignores him.

"This is between me and her," Don retorts.

"That may have been true, but the lady clearly doesn't want anything to do with you. You're making an ass of yourself right now," Chase counters.

Don instantly rises from the booth, sizing Chase up. I'm too shocked and scared to move or say anything.

"Pussy, get your bitch ass the fuck out of my face before I fuck both you and this cheap hoe up," Don hisses.

Without saying a word, Chase swings, punching Don square in his face. The impact is astounding, taking Don by surprise. His head snaps back, and suddenly, he's on the floor, knocked out cold.

"Oh my god!" I exclaim.

Bar security rushes over to us in an instant, immediately tending to Don, and forcing me and Chase to leave. Outside, I nervously pace back and forth; my hands are shaking.

"Chase, I am so sorry about that!"

He shakes his head, cool as a cucumber, "You don't have anything to apologize for. That dude was a dick; he had it coming."

"Thank goodness you were here. What's that twice in one week?" I ask.

Chase nods, "I'm glad that I was, who knows what that jerk would've pulled."

My body instantly shivers from the thought of what could've happened if Chase wasn't there to help me.

"Do you come here often?" I ask, trying to change the subject.

"Only a few times. I had a lot on my mind and decided to step out for a drink," he explains.

I look at Chase's hand which is badly swollen and bleeding. He must've cut his hand against Don's teeth. I quickly hail a cab and pull him inside with me.

The cab driver turns to me, "Where to?"

"Jefferson Place Apartments," I quickly say.

Ten minutes later, we're dropped off in front of my apartment building. I pull Chase out of the taxi and lead him to my place. Once there, I pull out my keys, using them to unlock the door.

"I'm ok, London; it doesn't hurt," he offers.

"You're bleeding. Let me clean you up; it's the least I can do," I say.

He nods, obliging me.

"Have a seat. I'll be right back," I say before disappearing into my bathroom.

"You have a really nice place," I hear him call out from the living room.

When I come back, he's standing in front of my fireplace, looking at pictures of me and my sister.

"Never would've guessed that there were two of you," he says.

"Yup," I smile.

I take a seat on the couch and pat the cushion at my side. He takes a few steps, joining me on the couch.

"I'm fine, really," he offers.

"Shh, hold still," I order.

I take a wet rag, wiping his cut clean. I swiftly follow up using a cotton ball and rubbing alcohol to disinfect his wound. He doesn't even flinch, just waits patiently as I attend to him.

"Thank you for defending me," I say.

"Don't mention it," he replies.

I put some ointment on the cut and follow up with a bandage.

"Are you sure you're ok?" he asks me again.

I nod, "Yes. All done."

"Thank you," he says.

I wink, "Don't mention it."

Chase sinks back into the couch and looks at me. Suddenly, he pulls me to him, kissing me softly on the lips. I pull away, completely shocked at first, but then I lean into his space, kissing him back. He gently places his hand on the nape of my neck. Suddenly to my dismay, he quickly pushes me away.

"I'm sorry. I shouldn't have done that," he murmurs.

"Then why did you?" I ask.

"That's something I've wanted to do since you walked into my classroom. I get that that's completely unethical and inappropriate," he admits.

My heart skips a beat.

"What if I don't care about any of that," I ask, surprising myself.

Before he can protest, I climb on top of him. As soon as I do, his lips, hungry with desire, are back onto mine. The attraction that I've always tried to ignore comes to the surface. I kiss him deeply, allowing myself to get lost with his tongue, his taste, and his smell.

Chase's hands gently rub the small of my back before softly moving to my waist and thighs.

I close my eyes and smile as my fingertips feel his chest through his shirt. Seductively, I whip my hair to the side and trail my tongue along his strong neck and jawline. I can feel him growing in his pants and begin grinding my hips into his solid erection. He reaches up, slowly unzipping my dress before making me stand up and pulling it to the floor. I stand there for a moment, bare, yearning to feel him inside of me.

Reaching out, he pulls me closer to him, tenderly kissing my belly then moving to my thighs. I gasp when he pulls down my panties and lifts one of my legs onto the couch. My skin tingles when I feel his mouth on my honeypot. My knees buckle as his tongue swirls against my clit. The cool sensation of his breath against that sensitive spot makes my head spin. I hold onto his shoulders, tossing my head back in pure ecstasy. I feel my intense release slowly building. To my astonishment, he delicately slips his middle finger inside me, and I pant with pleasure. I can barely contain myself when I suddenly feel two fingers gliding in and out.

After I climax, Chase swoops me up off of my feet and carries me into the bedroom. He's pleased to see my naked body on full display before taking off his own shirt and pants. Our eyes lock when he gets on top of me. I spread my legs, opening myself to him. As he enters me, I sensually bite my lip.

"You drive me crazy when you do that," he says.

He softly palms my breast as I moan in pleasure. I pull him closer to me, completely engulfed in our passion. His tongue traces my lips before getting lost with my own. I kiss him deeply, tasting my sweet nectar. It's as if time stops and nothing else matters. It's just me and him; we get lost in each other for the rest of the night.

# OLIVIA

**FORMER TEACHER CONVICTED OF ATTEMPTED MURDER IN SCANDALOUS MURDER SCHEME**

The bold headline pops against the cover of my fresh copy of the *Philadelphia Inquirer.* I anxiously flip through its pages, hoping to find an update on London's case. After countless stories, I come up short. Frustrated, I reach for my cappuccino and take a long sip.

There has to be something that I'm missing. I pull out my cell and go to the texts between me and London, desperate to find a clue. I scroll and scroll and scroll, but nothing stands out. Maybe I missed something on her social media. Next, I pull up her Instagram page. She definitely lived her life, but yet again, nothing that reveals any obvious clues.

Hopefully, Shay will have something that is useful because I am beginning to lose hope. I eagerly check the time; it will be another five or so minutes before she arrives. After meeting at the funeral, we bumped into each other once more. I invited her to meet me here. According to her, she was London's neighbor and friend, maybe she has a clue that will help.

"London? I never thought I'd see you in a place like this," an unfamiliar voice says.

I look up from my phone and am met by a stunningly gorgeous woman. She's extremely elegant, even in blue jeans. Before I can stop her, she gives me a hug.

She continues, "I know that you're probably still pissed at me for what happened at Rogue. But I swear, I didn't put anything in your drink; that girl was lying."

*Ok, now I'm confused.*

"Umm, I don't know how to tell you this, but London passed away over a week ago," I explain.

As soon as I utter the words, her eyes grow big, "What? How?"

"She was murdered," I say.

"My God, but you look identical," she says, as tears roll down her cheek.

I swallow hard, fighting back my own tears, "I'm Olivia, her sister."

She nods, "I'm so sorry. I can only imagine what you're going through."

The woman takes a seat, joining me at my table.

I sniff, "Thank you, but who are you?"

"I'm Stormy; your sister was an acquaintance," she explains.

I can't help but notice the hesitation in her voice. Maybe she knew something about London, something that could help.

"Do you know anything that might help the police? What were you saying about her drink? Who is lying? Did London have any enemies? Was she dating anyone?" I ask, shooting my questions out like an AK-47.

She looks surprised by my last question, "Why do you ask?"

I shrug, "Why wouldn't I?"

She stares at me for a moment, unsure of what to say.

"I mean, in our line of work, there are certain risks," Stormy mutters.

My eyebrow shoots up, "Your line of work?"

Stormy nods, "Yes, we provide experiences for men."

*What the hell does she mean experiences for men?*

Suddenly, my head spins. London did live an affluent lifestyle. According to her, she made great tips as a masseuse. I never questioned it because I never thought she had a reason to lie. I guess I was wrong.

"Like, an escort?" I finally say.

She nods, "She never told you?"

I shake my head, "No."

Stormy is instantly apologetic, "Sorry you had to find out like this."

I drag my fingers through my hair, trying to process the bomb that was just dropped on me.

"It's not your fault. I'm realizing that I didn't know my sister as well as I thought I did. We all have secrets, I guess," I rationalize.

"Oh girl, I've got a ton," Stormy says.

"Did she ever say anything about an upset client or something?" I question.

Stormy shakes her head again, "No, we weren't exactly close. We shared a mutual friend. She, wow."

"Wow, what?" I pry.

She looks concerned, "It seems like everyone that I know is dying."

Just then, her phone rings.

"I'm so sorry. I have to go," she says, rising from the chair.

I try stopping her, "Wait, what do you mean, everyone you know is dying?"

Stormy backs away, toward the door, "I'm really sorry."

Before I can stop her, she dashes out of the cafe in a hurry. I watch her as she treks towards a fire red BMW, coincidentally bumping into Shay before she reaches it.

"Stay the fuck away from me, you crazy bitch!" she sneers.

Shay looks astounded by the verbal attack, and rightfully so. Stormy was completely out of line, but before I can interject, she hops into her car and pulls off.

"Are you ok?" I ask Shay.

She quickly nods, "Yes, I'm fine."

"What was that all about?" I question as we head back to my table.

"I have no idea," she says.

I shrug and sit down, "Well, thank you for meeting me."

"It's the least that I could do," she smiles.

We get another order of coffee, my treat, before sitting back down and getting to business.

"I'm sure you already talked to the police," I begin. "But do you have any other information that might help them solve my sister's murder?"

Shay takes a sip of her latte and then says, "I'm sorry, I don't. I shared everything that I know with the police already."

I sigh, burying my face into my hands for a moment, "You said that you two were friends; nothing else comes to mind?"

She sits back into her chair, recollecting her thoughts for a minute, "I guess there's one thing."

"What is it?"

"She was always in the presence of bad company," Shay replies.

~

The next day, I wander along Kelly Drive. It's an unseasonably warm day, and I want to take advantage of the mild temperatures. The outside air feels good, fresh. I'm hopeful that it will help me find some clarity.

One thing that I now know plays over and over again in my head. London, my sister, slept with men for money.

I don't know why, or for how long, but I have a feeling it's the reason why she is dead. I want to tell Andrews, but I'm afraid that if I do, I'd be betraying her. She obviously didn't want anyone to know about this, not even me.

Various runners and people on their bikes pass me along the skinny pathway.

*What do you want me to do, London?*

Before I can make sense of my thoughts and how I will handle the situation, I see him. He's blended in with the other runners coming right towards me, but I haven't forgotten his face. Moments later, his eyes settle on me, and he comes to a halting stop.

Much like at the funeral, he turns and starts running in the opposite direction. I seize the moment to follow him, eager to get some answers.

"Hey!" I call out.

He keeps running.

"Stop! I want to ask you some questions!" I pant.

He crosses the street, and I am hot on his tail before a car speeds by, stopping me in my tracks. Mystery man gets away once again. I don't know who he is, but I know that he knows something.

*Why is he so hellbent on avoiding me?*

~

Later that evening, I walk into the police precinct and ask to speak to Detective Andrews. The receptionist picks up the phone and calls him. I can hear him instruct her to escort me back to his office. I walk in silence, but when we get there, he's nowhere to be seen.

She turns to me, "He'll be with you in a moment. Have a seat."

I watch her leave but opt to stand. Instead, I anxiously pace the floor of Andrew's office.

Moments later, he comes in.

"Detective Andrews, sorry to pop up on you like this," I say.

"Please, call me Brian," he insists.

I nod, "Brian. How are you guys coming along with the case?"

He looks worried, "I can assure you that we're doing all that we can."

"Have you arrested anyone? Any suspects?" I quiz.

Andrews coolly takes his seat, "We have some people we're looking into."

"Who?"

"I can't share that information right now," he admits.

I approach the chair next to his desk and slowly sit down, "I have something to tell you."

"What's going on?"

He pulls out his trusty notepad, prepared to take notes down.

My heartbeat quickens, and my palms become sweaty. I want to tell him, but the thought of betraying London makes me nauseous.

Instead, I say, "I keep running into this strange man. I think that he knows something."

Andrews jots down some notes, "Where have you seen him?"

I sigh, "At Lon's funeral, he looked...suspicious, out of place. Then I saw him again yesterday. When he saw me, he ran in the other direction. I chased him down."

The moment that I describe what happened, Andrews looks at me, clearly disapproving of my behavior.

He says, "I know that you want to find your sister's killer, and believe me, we're going to get them, but please, leave the police work to me."

For some reason, I become annoyed, "Well I can't help myself. Every time I speak to you, you don't have any answers."

He keeps his cool, "Anything else?"

Now I'm pissed, "Do you even care about finding my sister's killer? Every time I come in here, this whole department is preoccupied with doing better things like fucking browsing Facebook or jerking off."

At this point, I'm fuming, unable to hide my frustration.

"Solving this case is just as important to me, as it is to you, Olivia," he says.

"Oh, yeah? Why's that?" I challenge him.

"Because I know how losing someone that's close to you feels, and I know how much this means to you," Brian says.

I feel nervous again.

He continues, "I can assure you that I'm doing the best that I can, Olivia, but a few things came up that are a concern, I'll admit."

"Concern? Like what?"

"Your mother, for one," Brian says.

My skin grows hot.

"My mother? What the fuck does that have to do with anything?" I charge.

"Your mother is Zola Burrows, correct? That same Zola Burrows was convicted of murdering Terrance Phillips seventeen years ago. We can't rule out the possibility that this was retaliation."

By now, I am boiling, "Why the fuck are you bringing our mother into this?"

"You should've told me," he says, his voice is low.

"Go to hell!" I say, before storming out of the police station.

# LONDON

*Thursday, June 13, 2019*

Summer classes are about to start, and although I should be enjoying my last few days of freedom, I feel bizarre. I haven't seen or talked to Chase since the night we had sex, and I'm not sure if that's a good or bad thing. I've tried relentlessly to erase that night from my mind, but I fail miserably each time. My lips tingle at the memory of his tasting mine. My body becomes hot, remembering his hands caressing my skin. I want to call him, to send him an email, but every time I start to, I stop myself.

*Where can this go?*

He thinks that I'm a masseuse just trying to pay her way through college, for goodness sakes. I feel terrible for lying to him. What would he think if I told him the truth? 'Hey Chase, I like you and all, but there's one thing that I forgot to mention. I get paid to sleep with men for a living.' He just wouldn't understand.

Yes, he tried reaching out to me once grades were published for my final. I got an A, just in case you were wondering.

The email said something like, 'Great work, you've been such a pleasure as a student, London. I look forward to seeing what you do next.'

I'll admit, I reread that email about ten times, trying to dissect the true meaning or message behind it.

*Is he thinking about me as much as I'm thinking about him?*

"Porsha? Is everything alright?" Omar asks, ripping me from my mental torture.

"Huh?" I look at him, baffled.

"I said, is everything alright? You seem a bit distracted," he observes.

"I'm sorry, babe. I just remembered that I forgot to set the alarm at my apartment, that's all," I lie.

I reach out, softly palming his cheek.

"Oh, yeah, I've done that before. You should probably get the surveillance on an app on your phone, just to give you peace of mind, you know?" he suggests.

I nod, "That's a great idea. I'll look into it. But enough about that, tell me all about your trip to Napa. How was it?"

This is my reality. The best I can do is to completely forget about that night. That would be better for all of us.

~

*Friday, June 14, 2019*

My phone rings, indicating a new text.

**RICHARD: HEY. FREE FOR DINNER TONIGHT?**

I stare at my phone, contemplating my reply. Moments later, I hear a knock at my door.

"Oh my God, Liv!" I say in complete shock.

We share a long hug.

"What are you doing here?"

It's not that I'm not ecstatic to see her, it just isn't like her to drop in without a call. Especially now that she lives so far away.

"I missed you," she reveals.

I look down and notice a small suitcase in her hand. We hug once more. When we pull away, I examine her more closely. She looks different. Beautiful of course, but frazzled, fragile and alarmingly skinny. No kidding, the girl looks like she barely weighs over a hundred pounds.

"Everything ok? Why didn't you call me and let me know you were coming?" I ask.

She nods, "Yeah, believe it or not, I got a little homesick. I wanted to surprise you."

"See, I knew you'd miss Philly," I tease.

She smirks and follows me over to the couch.

I take a seat, "How long are you staying?"

"Just a couple of days, is that ok?" she asks.

"Girl, what? Of course. I'm just shocked that you're not here with Marcus," I observe.

Liv rolls her eyes, "No, not this time."

"Everything alright?"

"I'm fine, really," Liv assures me.

I'm not buying it; something is wrong, I can feel it.

*What's her deal?*

Before I try to dig for more answers, I quickly type up my text and hit send.

**LONDON: SORRY BABE I CAN'T MAKE IT TONIGHT.**

~

*Sunday, June 16, 2019*

The sun is high and bright. Its rays bounce off of my porcelain plates. I lift up my knife and fork, cutting into the last bit of my challah French toast. As I take a bite, I keep my eyes on Liv. She's standing a few feet away, on the phone. I don't know what she's talking about, but I do know that she looks pretty upset.

"You left me no choice," she argues.

I shift in my seat; this can't be good.

*Is Marcus the motivation behind this so-called random visit?*

"I'll be back this evening," she sighs. "Ok, bye."

Liv grips her phone and silently takes her seat, rejoining me at our table.

"Are you going to tell me what's going on with you?" I ask.

Liv stays silent, opting to pick up her mimosa and finish it off.

"Come on, Liv, I hate when you shut down like this. You know that you can talk to me about anything. Are you and Marcus having problems?" I pry.

Her silence is deafening. I hate it when she flatlines. She hasn't been this bad since we were teenagers. Frustrated, I reach for my mimosa and take a long sip. Liv exhales a deep breath before tucking her hair behind her ear.

Moments pass before she finally reveals, "Marcus has been really jealous lately."

"Jealous? You're a saint!" I say.

"According to him, I'm not. He says that I'm sneaky and hiding something from him," she continues.

"Sounds like an insecure guy to me, and those are the worst types of men to get involved with," I say.

"He's not insecure, Lon. Marcus is just protective, that's all," Liv counters.

I can tell that her eagerness to defend him only means that he has his hooks deep into her. I hate to see it. If only Liv knew her power; she wasn't always like this. I miss the strong Olivia, the one that wouldn't back down from anyone.

I shrug, "Ok, but are you happy?"

She snorts and it's clear that I've struck a nerve, "What kind of question is that?"

"I'd say a simple one."

"Can I get you anything else ladies?" Our server asks, briefly interrupting our heated conversation.

"We'll take another round, thank you," I say.

"Another?" Liv frowns.

I refuse to back down, "Yes, you clearly need it."

She giggles, but it is strained, forced.

I opt to change the subject, "You going to visit mom before you leave?"

Her eyebrows furrow again, "I hadn't planned on it."

"When's the last time you've seen her? I know she'd love to see you. She's always asking about you," I say.

She shrugs, "I don't know."

Now my patience is wearing thin. It's one thing to be tight-lipped about her relationship, but to blatantly avoid our mother after all that she's done for the both of us is completely unacceptable.

"Look, I get that whatever you're going through is something you're not willing to share, but you're being very distant. We're sisters; that's our mother. How can you pick up and leave town with no plans to see her?" I lecture.

"I don't want to talk about this right now."

"Well, when dammit? I'm tired of tiptoeing around you all of the time!" I vent.

Just then, our waitress returns with our mimosas.

Liv turns to her, "We'll take the check, thanks."

The waitress nods, promptly turning on her feet and excusing herself. I am sure that the tension between Liv and me could be cut with a knife.

Later that afternoon, I stroll through Temple's campus alone. I need to pick up a book for my Statistics class and figure I'd blow off some steam. Let's just say that Liv's still pissed at me; she barely said goodbye when I dropped her off at the airport a little over an hour ago.

I could sit and ponder for hours, playing out different possibilities and scenarios and what could be wrong, but I know that my speculation will get me nowhere if she remains so closed off. One thing that I know for certain is that it has everything to do with Marcus.

What I can't forgive is her determination to keep our mother out of her life. Like, how dare she! I mean, our mother is definitely flawed, and our childhood was far from easy, but our mother has done everything she could to make up for her mistakes, even making the ultimate sacrifice so that we could have a future. Olivia's treatment of her is not only heart-breaking but also disappointing.

I walk towards the Statistics aisle and pull out my phone, careful to confirm the exact title and edition of the book I'd need for the next six weeks. My eyes scan the shelf until I see *Statistics for Psychology: 3rd Edition*, and I grab it. Pleased, I suddenly want to get some college memorabilia.

*Why not?*

After paying nearly two hundred dollars for a book and sweatshirt, I grab my shopping bag and head towards the exit. Just as I do, I see him. Chase is standing less than ten feet away from me. He's preoccupied, looking through a small book of some sort. I'm immediately apprehensive.

*Should I say something?*

*How long has he been here?*

*Gosh, why did I have to sleep with him?*

It feels like a million questions are running through my mind. Just as a million more are about to start, he notices me. Frantic, I rush out of the store's exit.

Back at home, I'm cuddled up on the couch watching *Love Jones*.

My phone goes off, and I quickly pick it up.

**LIV: HOME.**

Although I'm still upset with her, I'm relieved to know that she got home safely.

**LONDON: THANKS FOR LETTING ME KNOW. I'M SO HAPPY YOU CAME, I LOVE YOU.**

*Olive branch, Olivia, olive branch.*

**LIV: LOVE YOU TOO.**

I smile and put my phone back down to reach for my bowl of lightly buttered popcorn. Well into the movie, I'm damn near in tears. I love a good love story. Darius and Nina's sultry tale is definitely one of my favorites. Things were just beginning to get hot and heavy between them when suddenly, I hear a knock at my door. I place the movie on pause and stand up to open it. When I do, I'm taken aback.

"Chase? What are you doing here?"

He looks tormented, confused even. I guess me bolting out of the bookstore and straight to my car as soon as we made eye contact didn't sit right with him.

"Why did you leave like that?" he says.

I nervously cross my arms in front of my chest, "I, I don't know. I wasn't expecting to see you." I admit, looking to my feet. "I guess I kind of panicked," I confess.

"I don't want you to feel that way. Don't feel like you have to go the other way when you see me. I didn't like it," his voice is strained.

I sigh, "I'm sorry. I wasn't expecting this."

"Can I come in?"

I nod, before stepping to the side. Once he walks in, I gently close the door behind him.

"Why didn't you call me? I know that you have my number or email," I blurt out.

"I was afraid that I came on too strong. I'm your teacher, London. I have violated all of the ethical codes. I just didn't know what to say or do," Chase explains.

"I can't stop thinking about the other night," I reveal.

"I'm sorry about that," he says.

Standing there in front of him, my feelings become crystal clear. I really like him, yet I don't really know him, and he has no clue about who I really am. For some reason, I don't care. And that scares the shit out of me. The realization is overwhelming. I feel out of control.

"I'm not," I finally say.

My admission makes me feel flushed. I can feel the redness of my cheeks. Embarrassed, I timidly look to the floor, crossing my arms in front of my chest.

*What am I doing?*

Chase reaches out his hand and touches my chin, forcing me to meet his gaze, "I lied. I'm not sorry."

The fluttering of my heart doesn't slow, "How do we do this?"

"Beats me, kiddo," he smiles.

My mind races, again consumed by the nagging curiosity about where this can truly go. Before I can say anything, Chase kisses me, forcing me to quiet the whispers of my fears.

I can't keep my hands off of him. His initial apprehension has completely faded away, and so has my own. I toss my arms around his shoulders as he reaches around and squeezes my behind firmly, pulling me closer.

Moments later, I lead him to my bedroom before pushing him down onto my mattress. He lies back and watches me slip off my silk teddy with lust in his eyes.

"You're the most beautiful woman I've ever seen," he breathes.

I smile as I join him on the bed. He pulls off his t-shirt as I tug off his jeans and boxer briefs. My naked body straddles his as I stare into his eyes. He sits up, brushing his lips lightly against mine, before reaching up and running his fingers through my hair. I can feel the hardness of his member grow against my womanhood. I gently roll my body, rubbing against it.

Completely aroused, Chase sensually bites on my bottom lip, "I've been wanting to do that too."

My thighs grow wetter with every second that passes between us. I kiss him once more, allowing my tongue to slowly dance with his. As we do, I slightly lift my hips and slide on top of him. He lies onto his back once more and firmly grips my waist as I ride him. My hands hungrily rub his chest, and my pelvic muscles tighten around his dick. I rock and swirl my hips to the sweet music of our lovemaking.

"You feel so good," I moan.

The heat between us is undeniable. My nipples stand at complete attention as he places one, then the other delicately into his mouth. My head spins, consumed by the smell of his cologne. I know that I will explode at any moment. Chase then trails his tongue across my chest then to the nape of my neck, using one hand to slightly pull on my hair and the other to smack my ass. The stinging sensation is electric. I get lost in every stroke, each one feeling deeper and better than the last.

"I'm about to cum," I cry.

As soon as I say the words, Chase simultaneously lifts his pelvis into me, and he pulls my hips up and down on top of him. My walls flex and stretch to his penis. Suddenly, I have an out-of-body experience, one of the most intense orgasms I've ever experienced in my life, and I feel like I'm floating.

"Oh fuck," he says.

We both climax before sinking back into the bed, completely exhausted and drunk with passion.

# OLIVIA

The morning air is cool, and the water is calm. February is coming to an end, meaning that spring is just around the corner. I keep my pace as I run along the Schuylkill River. The sun is just beginning to rise. I take a moment to stop and admire the soft rays of light creeping over the skylines, waking the city up.

Another night, another nightmare. I tossed and turned, thinking about everything. My demons refuse to grant me peace or sleep. Frustrated and anxious, I just threw on some sweats, grabbed my running sneakers and rushed out of my hotel room.

The trail is filled with early risers and some of the city's homeless, who are lying on top of makeshift beds under trees and covered walkways. I focus on my breathing and try to clear my mind. It's been a long while since I've gone for a nice run. Despite the frigid weather, it feels great to do something that is so familiar to me. My stride has slowed a bit, but I'm certain that I can get it back in no time. Running is good; it helps me escape. It helps me forget. I make a mental note to continue to do this along with booking an appointment with a therapist, perhaps. These last couple of days, I've realized that I have a lot of shit to sort through.

As I approach Center City, I pick up my pace. The harder I run, the more I try to sort through my mess of a life. My mind bounces from London to Marcus, to my mother, to Brian. Brian, whom I've suddenly realized I'm very attracted to. Sheesh, what a fucking shit show. I would fall for the person that's supposed to solve my sister's case. In addition to that, I've killed a man, and he knows about my mother, my past.

*How the hell is that supposed to work?*

But no matter how much I try to fight it, I can't ignore the butterflies I feel when I think of him or see him. I don't know if it's pure attraction or guilt for lying to him. Ever since finding out the truth about London's double life, I've been tormented with this information. Do I honor my sister and keep her secret safe? Or do I share something that she obviously didn't want anyone to know, with the hope that it will help the police find her killer? Memories of our childhood quickly flash in my head. I remember the last time I honored London's secret, even though I knew I should've told someone. Keeping that secret did much more bad than good.

Suddenly, I slip and fall. The impact is shocking and hard. I guess while I was busy trying to sort through all that, I failed to see the huge patch of black ice directly in my path.

"Ouch!" I cry out.

Completely embarrassed, I quickly check to see if anyone saw my fall of shame. Luckily, no one else is around. But just as I am about to continue with my run, I see something move. I notice them, trying to hide behind a tree some sixty yards away. They're wearing a black jacket and baseball cap, making it hard to see their face. I try my best to keep my cool and pick myself up from the ground. Instead of panicking, I start jogging again, but as I do, I can hear them running too.

*Are they following me, or am I being paranoid?*

My heart begins to race, and I pick up the pace. I quickly scan my surroundings, looking for a way to quickly avert my possible stalker.

I swear that I can hear them getting closer, but I continue forward, quickly taking a sharp left off the trail and into the pedestrian streets. My eyes grow big when I see my assailant's shadow drawing near, causing me to panic.

Along the parkway, the morning rush is beginning, making traffic super hectic. Cars speed by with drivers anxious to reach their destinations. Adrenaline courses through my veins, propelling me forward into the street. A few cars come to a screeching halt, beeping their horns and yelling profanities in my direction. Once I'm on the other side of the intersection, I quickly look over my shoulder, but they're gone.

*Unknown*

Killing someone is one of the most exhilarating feelings I've had in my entire existence. It's been two weeks since I murdered that bitch, and I wish that I could do it again. I replay that night over and over again in my mind, getting high off it like a drug. But as more days have gone by, its impact is becoming less prevalent. I'm losing that tingly sensation I get every time I remember the look in her eyes as she died, the blood splattering onto my skin.

When I saw her sister again this morning, I knew what I had to do. She has to die. Seeing her reminds me of London all over again.

I almost had her. She won't be so lucky next time. I just have to keep watching her and wait for the right time to strike. It has to be well thought out and perfectly planned.

My heart pounds. I nearly got caught today. I can't let that happen again. I stare into the mirror, angry with myself. I slap myself across the face hard with disapproval. The poignant tingle feels good to me.

*I'm going to get her.*

I close my eyes, remembering the pure fear I felt from her. I need to see her bleed.

I slowly walk throughout London's apartment, looking for something new to add to my collection. I wanted something new to remember her by, a new token of some sort.

Moments later, I wander into her bedroom, lying down on the box spring. The memories hit me like open floodgates, causing me to chuckle.

Suddenly, I hear voices by the front door. I quickly sit up and look for somewhere to hide. I run into the closet and camouflage myself with London's designer wardrobe.

*What a materialistic slut.*

As the front door opens, I hear Olivia's voice. Unfortunately for me, she's not alone.

"I'm absolutely positive; someone was following me this morning, Brian," she says.

I hear him ask, "Are you sure?"

"Yes, I'm certain," she confirms.

"Did you get a good look at them at all?"

I hear her sigh, "No, it was still a little dark, and they were dressed in all black."

"Was it a male or female?" he quizzes.

"I don't know."

My shoulders relax a bit, relieved.

"Well hopefully you scared them off," he says.

*If only that were true.*

"Yeah, hopefully. Thanks for meeting me here," she says.

"Don't mention it. The forensics team finished up a few days ago. Figured you'd want to be the first to know," Brian says.

I can hear footsteps. I guess they're checking the place out. Once they reach the bedroom, they stop. I hold my breath, careful not to make a sound.

"I can't do this," Olivia cries.

"Hey, it's ok. I understand how hard this is for you," he assures her.

"I really appreciate all of your help, Brian. I know that I said some mean things the other day. I was just frustrated. But I wasn't being completely honest with you," she explains.

Brian asks, "What do you mean?"

"A few days ago I met a woman that knew London. She revealed something about her that I had no clue about."

"Ok, what is that?"

I hear her sigh, "She said that London was an escort, that she slept with men for money. I'm so sorry that I didn't tell you sooner. I guess I felt guilty for telling her deepest darkest secret, you know? But I realized that I couldn't live with myself if I kept something from you that would help you solve this and find her killer."

"I understand, thank you for telling me. This is the kind of information that I need," he says.

"I'm really happy that you're working on my sister's case. I know that you'll catch whoever did this," she says.

He replies, "That means a lot to me, Olivia, especially coming from you."

Goodness, they are pathetic. I snort to myself but stay quiet. Then I hear it, they're kissing.

# LONDON

*Saturday, November 10, 2018*

"I'm leaving my wife, Porsha."

I nearly choke on my martini, "What are you talking about, Mike?"

He meets my gaze, his eyes certain.

Mike says, "I am leaving my wife. I don't love her anymore. I want to be with you. I already told her this morning. It's done."

My head spins. This is getting to be too much. I mean, I have feelings for this man. I care for him. How could I not? He was my first. But I thought that the terms of our relationship were clear; he is messing up the arrangement.

"Can you say something?" he says, interrupting my thoughts.

I sigh, "Mike, baby, listen to me. You don't know what you're saying."

I reach over the table and softly touch his hand.

He shakes his head, "I know exactly what I'm saying. I love you, Porsha; you're all I think about. Tell me you love me."

I look at him once more, "Mike, you are my client; that's all this ever was. You're married. I don't love you, not in that way."

My heart races when I see the look on his face; it's like my words have knocked the wind out of his chest.

"But I thought you cared about me," he confesses.

"I do, Mike. You're an amazing man, and I love spending time with you. But you're married. Saying that you're leaving your wife is one thing but leaving her for me is ridiculous. What did you think I was going to say?"

His head drops, hanging low, "Don't do this to me, Porsha."

Small goosebumps form all over my arms. I slightly bite my lip before taking a deep breath, "I'm sorry, Mike. I can't see you anymore. Goodbye."

Before he can stop me, I rise from my seat and hurry out of the Zahav restaurant and quickly retrieve my car from the valet. Mike rushes outside, trying to stop me.

"Porsha! Please," he begs.

His pleas go ignored. I jump into my car and speed off.

Later that night, I toss and turn. My nerves are shattered, and I can't shake the unsettling feeling taking over my body. I inhale deeply and exhale, staring up at my ceiling. I try that a few more times, but it doesn't work. Agitated, I look over to my bedside clock. It's two fifteen in the morning. Restless, I sit up and get out of bed. I need a distraction. I'm sure some late-night television will do the trick. After getting comfortable on my couch, I grab the remote and power on the television. I spend the next few moments mindlessly flipping through the channels.

Just as I settle on an old episode of *I Love New York,* my cell rings. I reach over and grab it off the arm of the couch, and my heart sinks when I see Mike's name come across the screen. I feel awful for breaking things off, but I feel it's the only way. It's sad to see him taking it so hard. By the fourth ring, I sigh and slide right to answer, maybe he calmed down.

"Hey, baby," I say.

Mike stays silent. I just hear his uneven breathing on the other end of the phone.

"Mike? Is everything ok?"

Silence.

I pull my phone away from my ear to ensure the call is still connected, and it is.

"Hello?" I say once more.

"Stay the fuck away from my husband, or I'll kill you, bitch."

*Click.*

~

*Tuesday, October 29, 2019*

"No!"

I'm torn from my sleep, my bare body covered in a cold sweat. I quickly scan my bedroom and sigh. As I rub the sleep out of my eyes, I hear the toilet flush and bathroom light flicker off. Moments later, Chase walks into my bedroom, completely naked, the moonlight glistening against his chestnut-brown skin. Any panic that

I felt immediately dissolves once I lay my eyes on him. It feels like a dream, a good one. He rejoins me in bed, sliding in close to me and wrapping his arms around my body.

"Are you ok? I thought I heard you scream," he asks.

I nod, "Just a bad dream."

He leans down, kissing me softly on my lips "No more scary movies for you before bed then."

I softly giggle, "Yeah, that must be it." I lie.

These last few months have been nothing short of amazing. I'm really falling for this man. It's so scary and exciting all at once. Normally I'm not so quick to fall for someone, but Chase feels safe, and if I allow myself to admit it, too good to be true. I can talk to him about anything...well, just about anything.

My bad dream had nothing to do with the horror film we watched only a few hours earlier, but everything to do with my troubled past. I dreamt that Terrance was back. I could feel his disgusting hands on me, droplets of his sweat touching my body. The memory makes my skin crawl. I want to tell Chase but reliving it all is too painful.

In addition to that, I still have no idea how to tell him about my lifestyle. As much as I care for him , I have no clue where this is going. Hell, we're keeping our entire affair under wraps. Why would I risk losing it all when I don't know if there's a future for us?

Yeah, I still have a plan on getting out, but this was not a part of that. Shit, I haven't been seeing Richard or Omar nearly as much as I was before; that has to count for something, right?

I lay staring up at the ceiling, comfortable beside him, feeling his skin against mine. I don't know what I'm going to do, but I also know that I don't want this to end any time soon.

Suddenly, he reaches over to my nightstand, checking his phone. He smiles to himself and pulls me in for another kiss.

"Happy birthday, beautiful."

Later that day, I'd just gotten off the phone with Liv. This is our first birthday we're celebrating a part. Honestly, it feels strange. Moments later, I receive a text.

**INEZ: HAPPY BIRTHDAY! I MISS YOU LONDON. LET ME TAKE YOU OUT FOR YOUR BIRTHDAY, MY TREAT. XOXO**

I stare at my phone, contemplating my reply. Ever since Shay helped me realize that Inez and Stormy drugged me, I've cut off all ties. They both denied it, of course, but I'm not buying it. Stormy was known for drugging people. I've seen it with my own eyes.

Instead, my fingers type up a text message and hit send.

**LONDON: I WISH YOU WERE INSIDE ME RIGHT NOW.**

I blush, embarrassed by my forwardness and lie back onto my bed. The thought of him and his lips on mine arouses me. I slowly start to caress my body and legs before moving to my womanhood. Memories of his smell and the feel of his arms race through my mind. I continue to touch myself until I climax.

~

*Thursday, October 31, 2019*

"London, I know that you're in there. You can't ignore me forever!" Inez says outside my door.

Her words seem to be a bit slurred like she's drunk.

I open my door, and she's leaning against the wall in front of my door.

"What the hell are you doing?" I say.

She doesn't look good.

"You left me no choice; you won't talk to me!" she cries.

I look to my feet, "I'm still upset."

Inez cries, "London, I swear on my life, I would never do something like that. Drug you? You're like a sister to me."

My eyes water. I hate seeing her like this. She is a complete mess. I hear a door open then see Shay stick her head out.

"Everything alright, London?" I hear her say.

"Why don't you mind your business, Shay? London isn't your friend, she's mine, so back the fuck off!" Inez curses.

"Inez! Stop it," I shout. Then I turn to Shay, "I'm sorry, girl, can you please give us some privacy?"

Inez fumes, "No, you don't even know this chick! I bet you she's the one that drugged you! She's not your friend."

Shay looks visibly upset at Inez's attack. I can tell that she is fighting to keep her thoughts to herself.

She simply says, "Fine."

I cross my arms and watch her close her apartment door.

"What the hell is wrong with you, Inez? Why did you say that to her?" I ask.

"I don't like her or trust her, London, and neither should you," Inez replies.

I shake my head, "Look. We can talk, but I want you to be sober when we do, ok?"

Inez quickly nods, "Ok. How's tomorrow? I will send you the location."

"Alright, tomorrow works. It's a date," I confirm.

The next night at Attico, I'm sitting at the bar, a nervous wreck. I anxiously pick up my phone and try to call Inez for what feels like the hundredth time. But again, her phone just rings and rings before going to voicemail. This isn't like her. She wouldn't just blow me off like this, especially when we're on such rocky terms. Even though I am still a little pissed at her, I'm beginning to get worried.

I take a sip of my champagne and try to calm my nerves, but it doesn't help. I check my phone again, hoping to have missed a message from her, but still, nothing. I can feel a guy from across the bar watching me. He tries making eye contact, but I ignore his flirting, turning my back towards him and calling Inez again.

"Hey, you know who this is! I'm not able to answer my phone at the moment so leave me a message and make it good!" her voice sings out through the speaker.

"Inez, it's me, Lon. Is everything ok? I'm starting to get worried. Call me back when you get this," I say before hanging up.

*Something's not right.*

I take the last of my drink and attempt to calm my nerves. Inez is a big girl. I'm sure there's a logical explanation for this. I reason with myself that I'm probably overreacting and that it's time to go home.

The next morning, I wake up and instantly check my phone for any missed calls or messages, but to my dismay, nothing. I dial Inez again, but this time it goes straight to voicemail without ringing. My heart skips a beat, and I can't ignore the sick feeling growing in my stomach. I try to distract myself by turning on the television. As soon as I do, I nearly choke. I reread the news headline and scream.

**WOMAN, 34, MURDERED, THROWN OVER HOTEL BALCONY IN CENTER CITY PHILADELPHIA.**

A picture of Inez flashes onto the screen.

# OLIVIA

B*reathe in.*

*Breathe out.*

I'm sitting Indian style on the floor, trying to coach myself into relaxation, but my thoughts won't settle. I open my eyes and look down at the picture in my hand. It was taken nearly twenty years ago, of me, London and our mother. I sigh; the day this photo was taken, life was so much simpler.

Memories of going to London's apartment the day before play over in my mind. It was way harder than I could have ever imagined. As soon as I walked in, I was overwhelmed. Seeing her belongings, pictures of her; it even smelled like her. Thank goodness Brian was there with me to help me through it. It felt good to tell him the truth. One minute I'm devastated, crying about London and then the next moment, we're kissing. My stomach flips just thinking about it.

*Knock!*

*Knock!*

My eyes dart toward my hotel room door. Brian greets me with a smile once I open it. He looks happy, hopeful, something that I rarely see from him. Usually, he's so guarded and hard to read. It's nice to see him this way. I like it. Deep down, I can't stop myself from wondering if I had anything to do with it.

He walks into my room, and I follow, closing the door behind us.

"What's up?" I ask, trying to remain casual.

Brian is beaming, "We got him! We got our guy, picked him up this morning."

I can't believe my ears, "You got him?"

He nods.

"Who is he? How?"

"Chase Harris. We got an anonymous tip late last night. Apparently, he was having an affair with your sister for a few months," he explains, pulling a photograph out of his jacket pocket and handing it to me.

When I see his face, I recognize it immediately. This is the same guy that I've been running into recently. Turns out, he did have a reason to avoid me. The guilt was probably eating away at him and rightfully so.

"How do you know it was him?" I ask.

"We found DNA at her house that we haven't been able to match. When we took his sample, it was a perfect match. Also, witnesses say they saw him enter and leave the apartment in a hurry that night."

I'm exasperated, "So that's it? It's done?"

He nods with confidence, "Yes."

I sit down onto the bed, stunned. Part of me is elated, but another part can't believe that this is actually happening. I weave my fingers through my hair and softly rub my head, soothing some of the pressure I feel.

Brian sits next to me on the bed.

"So, now what?" I ask, turning to face him.

"What do you mean?" his eyebrows furrow.

"With the case," I say.

*And us.*

I want to know that our attraction is real, that I hadn't imagined it. But I can't ask; it's far too risky.

"We charge him, prosecute in court and hopefully, get a conviction," he says, interrupting my thoughts.

"Hopefully?" I ask.

I don't like that word. I want to know with one hundred percent certainty that this bastard will rot in jail for the rest of his life.

"Yeah, that's how it works, unfortunately," Brian shrugs.

"That doesn't bring my sister back," I say, frustrated.

He places his hand on my shoulder, "Hey, I get it, but this is good."

I nod.

He is right; this is a good thing. It's progress, a step forward, like he said. I refuse to let London die in vain. Having the man responsible for her death finally answer for his mistakes will assure that. I relax a bit, laying my head on his shoulder. My spirit feels a bit lighter than usual. I feel safe, something I haven't felt in a very long time.

"Thank you, Brian," I say.

He nods and gently places his hand on my knee, "I can't stop thinking about the other night."

"Neither can I," I admit.

I gaze into his eyes and place my hand on top of his, before lifting it and resting it gently against my cheek. His skin feels like warm silk.

"Kiss me," I whisper.

Brian doesn't hesitate. He gently moves his hand to the nape of my neck before placing his lips onto mine. I pull him against me, eager to get closer to him, to feel his skin on mine. My nipples stand at attention, poking through my white t-shirt, and I can feel the deep insides of my thighs grow moist. I pull on his tie, quickly undoing it and then move to his pants. When he removes his shirt, I slide his pants and briefs to the floor. My eyes grow big at the size of him.

He lifts me up, bringing me back to his level. I lie back onto the bed, pulling Brian with me. Our lips never lose touch. His hands move from my neck, down to my breasts, then to between my legs. I moan as his fingers strategically rub against my spot. After I climax, he reaches for a condom, ripping open the Magnum wrapper before sliding it on.

I gasp when he slips inside of me. With each thrust, I get lost in him and the scorching heat between us. I arch my back, pulling him deeper inside my water well. My tongue trails along his neck, then I slightly nibble on his ear. Brian runs his fingers through my hair as he continuously plunges into me.

"You're so wet," he whispers.

Those words make my skin tingle. My fingers dig into his back, and I bite my lip, preparing to explode.

"Shit," Brian says, as we both orgasm.

~

Later that evening, I reach for my compact mirror and check my lipstick, the cherry red shade that London once got me. It has been a while since I took the time to dress and get dolled up, but the news of Chase's arrest is a cause for celebration. When I called Avery with the good news, she insisted we go out for some drinks, and I couldn't agree more.

As I apply more lipstick, I wonder if I should come clean about my situation with Brian. Now that the arrest has been made, we may be able to continue whatever this is without all the secrecy. I know that I have no business even dealing with anyone, especially given my baggage and secrets, but I'm so drawn to him.

I grab my purse and hop out of my car before making my way into Sampan. The restaurant is elegant and hip, with modern Asian décor and flare. The crowd is small and modest, but I know that it is still a bit early. The evening crowd will be coming out soon, and this place will be packed to capacity. When I enter, I see Avery seated at a small table by the window, scanning the menu.

As soon as she sees me, her eyes light up, "Hey, girl! You look great."

"Thank you. It's been a while since I got cute like this, I'll admit," I say.

"I understand. You've been through a lot lately," she says.

We hug and take our seats. Moments later, we're joined by our waiter and promptly order a round of drinks and appetizers.

"How have you been? I haven't seen you since the funeral," I start.

Avery says, "I'm alright. Work has been hectic, but I wouldn't have it any other way."

I ask, "Did you ever find an assistant?"

She shakes her head, "No one is quite right. On the other hand, I did manage to go on a few dates, but nothing to brag about. Guys these days are just, eh."

We laugh as our waiter returns with our drinks and food.

I grab my glass and lift it up for a toast, "Well, here's to you slaying the event planning business and meeting your future soulmate."

Avery grabs her drink, mimicking my actions, "And here's to getting justice for London."

We tap our drinks and take a sip. Twenty minutes later, we're deep into conversation. I'm giving her the rundown on Brian.

"Wait, so he's a cop?"

I nod.

She takes another sip of her cocktail, "That's kind of hot."

I blush, amused and slightly embarrassed. When I glance out the restaurant window, I see Shay standing directly across the street. She's on her phone, pacing back and forth. I wave at her, trying to get her attention.

"What are you doing?" Avery asks, looking out the window in Shay's direction.

"I know that woman. She came to the funeral. She was London's neighbor," I explain.

Avery is shocked, "Do you know who that is?"

Just then, Shay turns on her heels, walking away.

I turn my attention back to Avery, "Am I supposed to?"

She shrugs, "I never forget a face. I planned an event for her and her husband once in Baltimore. She was all over the news a few years back. Her husband was this huge real estate broker or something. Anyway, he suddenly died one day, stroke or something. Police thought she did it for a while."

"What? That's crazy! And sad," I say.

Avery nods, "Yeah, they said that she went berserk when it all went down, chopped off all her hair like Britney Spears or some shit."

"No way! Damn, that's sad. She's really sweet from what I can tell," I say in complete shock.

Avery nods, "Yup, tell me about it. Sis is definitely batshit crazy."

I look up, "I would've never guessed."

# LONDON

*Tuesday, April 8, 2003*

I lie in my bed and stare up at the ceiling, watching the streetlights and shadows dance throughout my room. The effects of the Ibuprofen are beginning to wear off. The last few hours play over in my head like a movie. I remember the operating room being cold and hard, and lying on the operating table, wishing for a different life.

The front door to our house opens and shuts, only meaning mom has left for her overnight shift at the hospital. I reach for my CD player, putting my headphones in and turning on Aaliyah. I hum and snap my fingers to her angelic voice until I fall asleep.

Hours later, I hear him make his way towards my room. I take a deep breath and calm my nerves, fixating my eyes on my wall in front of me. The light from the hallway creeps in when he opens my bedroom door. My heartbeat quickens. The floor creaks under the weight of his footsteps, sending chills up my spine.

The sound of his pants and belt buckle hitting the wooden floor makes my skin crawl. When I feel his hand on my shoulder, I want to vomit. I keep my back towards him, refusing to look at him and hug tightly onto my pillow.

He tugs on me, with more force this time, making me turn over to face him. I try to scream, but his fat hand covers my mouth, muffling my cries.

Suddenly, I see a shadow of a figure standing behind him. My eyes widen when I realize it's my sister. Liv's there, trembling, holding a gun directly pointed at Terrance.

"Let her go," she orders, startling him.

He turns around, astonished, his hands in the air, seemingly exposed.

"Get the fuck away from her," she commands.

~

*Friday, January 17, 2020*

I put on my lipstick and adjust my graduation cap. The day is here, my graduation. After all the hiccups, mistakes, heartache, and stress, I can't believe that I'm actually graduating. Although I should feel completely ecstatic, I don't. I keep thinking about Inez and her untimely death. I'm so hurt that she's no longer here, especially to celebrate with me today. She had been in my corner and supported my decision to get my degree from day one. I close my eyes, imagining what she would be saying if she was here.

*"You go, girl! I knew you could do it!"*

I smile to myself and dot my tear ducts with a Kleenex. It's bittersweet. My phone rings.

**OMAR: I GOT YOUR MESSAGE. I WISH YOU LUCK IN YOUR FUTURE ENDEAVORS, PORSHA. IT'S BEEN A PLEASURE KNOWING YOU.**

I stare at my phone, feeling relieved. I can't believe that it's all over. Last night, after a few glasses of wine and lots of back and forth between my thoughts, I finally made the decision to hang up the towel. I'm no longer a woman that sleeps with men for money. I want love. I want a career. I want a family.

Losing Inez was a huge wake-up call. Although her case still remains unsolved, I have reason to believe that one of her clients murdered her. It makes the most sense, especially given that scary encounter that I had with that creep a few months back. Some men don't know how to take rejection and ultimately make their rejector pay the price. I hate that Inez ended up meeting this fate. She loved this life so much; it's a shame that it would be the same thing that killed her.

Another text comes through and I smile.

**CHASE: CONGRATULATIONS LONDON. I'M SO PROUD OF YOU & CAN'T WAIT TO CELEBRATE WITH YOU. I LOVE YOU.**

My heart feels full. I wish that he could be here with me. I spent so many nights imagining running off the stage and into his arms. Now that I'm no longer a college student, we can take our relationship public. No secrets, no lies, just us.

**LONDON: I LOVE YOU TOO.**

I quickly type up my message and hit send.

"You almost ready?" Liv calls out from the living room.

"Yeah, one minute," I say.

~

*Thursday, February 13, 2020*

My heels click against the hard, ceramic tile. I clutch my purse tightly, hurrying to my destination. I don't want to be seen. Luckily, it's after hours, and things are quiet, making it easy to be discreet.

He texted me earlier saying that he'd be in his office late today, grading papers. I spent my afternoon fantasizing about how sexy it would be if I showed up with a bottle of wine and let him take me right on top of his desk.

When I see his name displayed across his door, it sends butterflies through my stomach. I quickly run my fingers through my hair and open the door. As soon as I do, I see them kissing. Chase, and a woman that I've never seen before. The shock hits me hard, causing me to drop the bottle of Merlot I'd brought with me onto the floor. The thundering shatter of the glass catches their attention immediately. When Chase sees me, he is mortified.

"London, wait!" he calls out.

But he's too late. I'm already gone. I run out of the room and down the exit stairwell, nearly breaking my heels. Once I exit the building, I get into my car and drive.

Minutes pass before I finally pull over along Kelly Drive. With tears streaming down my face, I put my car in park and get out.

*How could I have been so stupid?*

*How did I miss the signs?*

A million questions run through my mind as I stare out to the riverbank. An hour or so later, I'm back at home. My elevator bell softly rings. I patiently wait for the doors to open before stepping out onto my floor. When I do, Chase is there by my door. He's seated on the ground with his head in his hands.

"What are you doing here?" I ask.

My voice startles him. He looks up and is relieved to see me.

"London, please let me explain," he begs.

Chase tries to reach out and touch me, but I step back, avoiding him.

I cross my arms over my chest, as if they're a shield, "Don't touch me. Just explain what's going on."

*That's the very least he could do.*

He rises to his feet, "Can we go inside and talk?"

I don't like the sound of this. I instantly feel sick to my stomach. I hear a door open and see Shay exit her apartment.

"Hey, London," she smiles.

"Hi, Shay," I reply.

She can sense the tension as she gets closer to us, "Everything ok?"

I nod, "Yes, everything is fine."

Her eyes go from me, then to Chase and then back to me.

Shay smiles, "Ok. Well, have a good night."

Chase and I watch her as she walks down the hallway and steps onto the elevator when it arrives. The last thing that I want is for my neighbors to know all of my business. I pull out my key, unlock my door and walk inside. He follows me, closing the door behind him.

I waste no time, "Who was that, and why were you kissing her?"

Chase jams his hands into his jean pockets, pacing, "That...that was my wife."

"Your wife? Are you serious? So, you just conveniently forgot to tell me that you were married?" I shout.

I check his ring finger. A wedding ring is something I could easily spot, but there's nothing there.

"It's not like that; we've been separated for over a year. We're getting a divorce," he explains.

I toss my purse onto my couch, "You two seemed pretty damn close to be getting a divorce."

He shakes his head, "We're not. I only invited her to my office because I had some things I needed to give her. When she arrived, I realized she'd been drinking. She kissed me, and that's when you walked in. Please believe me, London."

"Chase, you were kissing her just as much as she was kissing you," I challenge.

"I'm sorry. I fucked up," he says.

He walks towards me, with open arms, but I reject him.

"I love you, London," he says.

As I look into his eyes, I know that he means every word. I look at him, standing before me, settling in his truth. How can I be so mad at him when I've been lying to him myself? My breathing becomes ragged and uneven. I have to come clean.

I look to the floor and bite my bottom lip, "Since we're being honest with each other, I have something to tell you too."

Chase instantly appears concerned, my words throwing him for a loop. He walks over to my couch and slowly takes a seat.

I sigh, before joining him, "I haven't been completely truthful about what I do for a living. See, before I met you, I'd been through so much. I was down on my luck. It was bad. I was damn near homeless. Then one day, I was invited out on a date. At the end of the night, I made five hundred dollars."

Now his breathing is ragged. My eyes stay glued to the floor. I'm too afraid to see what they may say.

Finally, he says, "What are you saying, London?"

My lips quiver, "I'm saying that I was an escort."

Once I say the words, it's like the wind has been knocked from his chest. He leans back on the couch, sinking back into the pillows.

"You sleep with men for money?" he asks, so low I can barely hear him at first.

I sniff, "Yes, but that's over now. I ended all that when you and I got serious because I love you, Chase."

Moments pass before either of us say anything. All I can hear is the rapid beating of my heart. Just as I find the courage to say something, Chase rises to his feet and shakes his head.

"I'm sorry, I can't do this," he admits.

My eyes well with tears, "So, that's it? We're done? Just like that?"

Chase slowly nods, "Yeah."

Without saying another word, he hastily heads for the door, opening and softly shutting it behind him. Once he does, I allow the tears to stream down my face.

That night, I rip out of my sleep. My sheets are covered with my sweat, and my throat feels eerily dry. Suddenly, I feel violently nauseous. I jump up and run to the bathroom. I drop down onto my knees and hang my head into the toilet, throwing up my dinner. After a few dry heaves and deep breaths, I sit pressing my back up against the wall. Using my free hand to wipe my mouth, I try to regain my strength; my body appreciating the coolness of the bathroom tile.

*What a horrible fucking day.*

Then I see it, the unopened box of tampons. The tampons that I purchased with the intention of using weeks ago.

*I'm late.*

Panicked, I pull myself up off the ground and stare at myself in the mirror. I examine every inch of my body, turning from side to side and touching my belly. Without hesitation, I rush into my bedroom, throwing on my clothes in a hurry. Luckily, the pharmacy is twenty-four hours and only a few blocks away.

Back at home, I pace the bathroom waiting for the results and check my watch for what feels like the millionth time. Seconds feel like hours. I grip the pregnancy test and nervously chew on my nails.

*Beep!*

*Beep!*

*Beep!*

Finally, my timer goes off, and the results are ready. When I pick up the stick, I see the words PREGNANT bright and bold on the tiny digital screen.

# OLIVIA

The sun glimmers in my hotel room, waking me up. I slowly open my eyes. It's the calmest I've been in quite some time. The bedside clock reads a quarter past seven in the morning. I carefully stretch my arms up above my head. As I do, Brian turns over, wrapping his strong arms around my nude body.

"Good morning," he says before kissing my neck.

I smile and say, "Morning."

Brian pulls me on top of him, gently cradling my thighs, and I arch my back. We spent most of the night before love-making, but I don't care. I crave more.

A few hours later, I exit the shower and dry off my damp body. Just as I do, I can hear Brian's phone ring from the bedroom.

"Andrews," he answers.

I reach for my lotion and moisturize my skin.

"What the fuck are you talking about?" I hear him yell.

Concerned, I put on the white robe and step out of the bathroom to check on him. He's pacing the room in his boxers. He looks phenomenal, but I can tell whatever it is, it can't be good.

"Give me twenty minutes," he says before hanging up.

As he does, he tosses the phone onto the bed in frustration.

"Is everything ok?" I ask.

He takes a seat on the bed, burying his head into his hands. I've never seen him so upset before. I make my way over to him, sliding our room service tray out of the way before taking a seat beside him.

"Hey," I say, gently stroking his back.

When he looks up at me, he looks defeated.

"I'm so sorry," he says.

"Sorry? About what?"

He sighs and stands up, "Chase Harris was released this morning."

My eyes widen, "What? How? I thought you had his DNA."

Brian kneels down in front of me, "We did. We do. He was at your sister's that night, but not at the time she was killed. His estranged wife just came forward, confirming his alibi; he was with her at the time of the murder. She has surveillance footage with a timestamp."

"You're lying!" I scream. "He killed her! You said so! You promised that you'd get him! You promised me!"

I suddenly burst into tears; any hope or peace I was beginning to feel completely evaporates. We're back at square one. Brian tries pulling me in for a hug, but I push him away, rejecting him.

"Don't touch me!"

I can see that he's hurt by my words.

He rises from the floor and redresses in silence. Frustrated, I go to the window, staring out into the city. I cry as little snow flurries come down from the sky.

"I'll let you know when I have any updates on the case," he says.

I hear the front door open and close behind him.

Hours later, I hear a soft knock at the door, and I rise from the bed, slightly relieved. After shedding some tears and taking a few deep breaths, allowing my anger to subside, I realize that none of this is Brian's fault, and my anger towards him was unjust. I know that he's doing the best that he can to find my sister's killer. He's been really good to me, and I appreciate him for it. Feeling silly, I sent him a text apologizing and inviting him back over, but hours passed with no response.

*What if I pushed him away for good?*

I open the door and nearly faint. His eyes are as cold and menacing as ever. I want to scream, but I'm paralyzed. I'm not sure if this is real or if my mind is playing tricks on me.

"Hello, beautiful," the sound of his voice sends shock waves down my spine.

Marcus stares a hole through my soul. Before I can shut and lock the door, he overpowers me, pushing his way through and slamming the door behind him.

I try to scream, but he places his large hand over my mouth, silencing my screams. I kick and squirm, trying to free myself from him. During all of the commotion, he reaches into his pocket, pulling out a white rag and placing it over my nose and mouth. I try to resist him, but then I feel myself drift.

~

*Tuesday, April 8, 2003*

The front door opens, and our mother is home early. I can feel the adrenaline pulsing through my bloodstream. My knees are shaky, but I hold steady, keeping the gun pointed at Terrance. I watch his eyes dart towards the door in a panic. Moments later, I hear her enter the bedroom.

"Olivia! What the hell are you doing?" mom asks.

"I'm protecting my sister. I have to."

"Olivia, please don't do this. Tell me what's going on," my mother pleads.

She's so naïve. How can she not put two and two together, even still? If she isn't going to protect us, then I will.

"Why don't you ask your boyfriend what he's been doing to London while you're away at night," I say, keeping the gun pointed at Terrance.

"Zola, baby, please," he says.

Finally, my mother looks at him. His hands are up; his pants are down. And for the first time, my mother sees him for what he really is, a pedophile rapist.

"Do you know that he got London pregnant? She went and got an abortion today because he rapes her repeatedly," I reveal.

My mother cries, but I don't feel sorry for her. I watch London crying in the corner, ashamed.

"Tell her, London," I command.

"Is it true?" mom turns to her.

London turns over, wiping the tears from her eyes before taking a deep breath, "Yes, mom, it's true."

She rises to her feet and slowly places her feet onto the floor. I keep my eyes on Terrance as she stands up.

"Zola, baby, they're lying!" he pleads.

But my mother doesn't hear him, she's just crying. London makes her way toward us.

Just then, Terrance reaches out, grabbing her arm, "You bitch!"

*Bang!*

It all happens so fast, he falls back onto the bed gripping his chest. The smell of the smoke from the barrel fills my nose. I drop the gun to the floor in complete shock.

~

My eyes flicker. I feel myself come to and slowly open them. The room is still hazy, and I try to find something to focus on. My arms slightly tingle from their uncomfortable position. I look down and see my hands are tied behind my back. I panic, trying to break free from my restraints. I see my phone, the brass candle holder and what's left of the money I took lying on the bed.

Marcus walks into the living room, "Welcome back, sweetie."

He strokes my hair, and I flinch. He's amused by my reaction and takes a seat on the bed in front of me.

"We have quite a few things to discuss," he begins.

Angry tears run down my face.

"First, you left me for dead, and then you had the nerve to steal from me," Marcus recollects.

I keep my eyes on him but start to fiddle with my hands to loosen the rope looped around them.

"I'll let you speak, but if you so much as scream, I'll slit your fucking throat. Got it?"

I quickly nod.

Marcus carefully removes the rag from over my mouth.

"I thought I killed you," my voice shakes.

"You damn sure tried. Imagine how shocked I was when I suddenly woke up lying on the bathroom floor covered in blood, only to see that my girlfriend and my money were gone. I thought about calling the police and reporting your ass, but then I realized I'd have way more fun tracking you down and making you pay with my own bare hands."

A tight lump forms in my throat.

"How did you find me?" I manage to ask.

He laughs, "You're predictable and boring, Liv. I knew you'd come running to your sister."

I remain tight-lipped, instead, focusing on getting my hands loose.

"I was amused to find out she ended up getting herself killed. I've got to say, I'm not surprised. Whatever she did, I'm sure she had it coming," he hisses.

I scowl at his statement, nearly jumping out of my seat, "Fuck you!"

Marcus is unbothered, "Speaking of fucking, I noticed you've been hanging around with that cop too. You been fucking him?"

I stay silent.

Suddenly, he slaps me hard across my face, "Answer me, you fucking whore!"

Now he's enraged. He wraps his hands around my neck and starts to choke me. I feel myself blacking out but will myself to stay focused on undoing the rope which is starting to give way. Finally, my prayers are answered, and my hands come free. In an instant, I punch him right in his groin. Marcus is unfazed, keeping his grip around my neck. With gut-wrenching force, he throws me up against the wall, causing me to hit my head really hard.

My head throbs from the pain, but I refuse to give up. This time, I kick him in the balls and try gouging his eyes out, causing him to fall to the floor. While he's down, I make a run for the door and manage to get it open. But before I can reach safety, Marcus has a fistful of my hair, pulling me back and throwing me down onto the bed.

"You're going to die like your fucking sister, bitch," he threatens.

I try to scream, and he punches me in the face. The impact is so hard it nearly makes me choke on my own saliva. But I will myself to keep on fighting. I refuse to die here. I bite into his forearm, sinking my teeth into his flesh with all my might causing him to scream in pain.

"Help me! Somebody help me, please!" I manage to yell out.

Enraged, Marcus begins choking me. I toss and wriggle, trying to free myself yet again. Every time I do, his grip gets tighter and tighter. I know that it won't be long before I stop breathing. They say when you die, you see a light. That's bullshit because all I see is darkness. Cold, empty darkness.

*At least I'll be reunited with London.*

"Let her go!" I hear a voice say as the door bursts open.

Marcus ignores him, his hands gripping my neck more firmly.

*Bang!*

The blast from the gunshot rings loudly in my ear. Then I feel the weight of Marcus' body as he collapses on top of me. Brian is at my side at once, pulling me off the bed and securely behind him. Marcus rolls over in pain gripping his shoulder.

Brian brandishes his firearm once more, "Don't move!"

He quickly takes out his handcuffs before turning him over and detaining him. A few minutes later, more police officers arrive.

Marcus stares daggers at me when the cops escort him out of the room and haul him off to jail. I sit on the bed with my arms tightly wrapped around my body, trying to process the wild turn of events.

At the police station, it seems that time has slowed. Everything is moving at a snail's pace. I twist in my seat and watch the stillness of the wall, completely removed from my reality. More moments pass before a female detective enters the office.

She takes a seat at her desk, eyeing me carefully. I gently nibble on my finger, trying to anticipate the questions she may drill me with.

*Is she going to ask me questions about Andrews and how he was able to find me?*

*Oh God, I hope that I haven't gotten him in trouble.*

As my mind fills with panic, the detective opens a thin notepad.

"Do you know Jessica Daniels?" she begins.

I shake my head no.

Her face is unmoving, "How long have you known Marcus?"

"We were together for two years," I say.

She nods, as she scribbles something down, "Has Marcus ever been physically abusive towards you in the past?"

I nod, embarrassed.

"Have you ever reported it?"

I shake my head no with shame again.

She sighs, "Well, I have to say, Ms. Burrows, you're one lucky girl."

Now she has my attention.

"Excuse me?"

"We have reason to believe that Marcus murdered his ex-girlfriend over a year ago. I'm glad to see that you didn't meet the same fate as her," she smiles.

I sit there, dumbfounded.

*How could I be so naïve?*

Small goosebumps cover my forearms. I'm so lucky to still be alive. The realization is too much to comprehend. I take a deep breath and start to cry.

She reaches out her hand, placing it on top of mine, "It's safe to say that he'll be going away for a long time. You're safe now."

~

My hand slightly trembles as I slowly reach out and knock on the door. Moments later, Brian answers the door shirtless and looking godlike; he's relieved to see me. I couldn't bring myself to go back to my hotel room and didn't want to be alone, not tonight. Once I step inside, he closes the door behind me and instantly pulls me in for a hug.

"You saved my life," I cry.

He gently wipes away my tears, "And I would gladly do it again."

I sniff and take a deep breath, "Thank you."

Brian takes my hand and leads me into the living room. I see two glasses of red wine on the table.

"I figured you could use it after the day you had," he says.

I chuckle a little and join him in his living room. When he hands me my drink, I take a long sip and admire his condo. Seconds later, I walk over to his bookshelf and quickly explore all of his pictures. I see what looks like a recent picture of Brian and an older woman. He has her eyes and cheekbones.

"Your mother is beautiful," I compliment.

Brian stands back, watching me, "Thank you."

"Any siblings?"

Then I see them; it's Brian, about ten or fifteen years younger, holding a basketball and sporting a boyish grin, alongside his identical twin.

I quickly pick it up and look at Brian, who is now by my side.

"My brother, Brandon. He was murdered fifteen years ago," he reveals.

"I'm so sorry, Brian. So when you said that you knew what I was going through..." I say.

He finishes my sentence, "I meant it."

I take his hand into mine and gently kiss it before putting the photo down, back in its place.

"No crazy wives or girlfriends I should know about?" I tease, in an effort to lighten the mood.

I hear him snort, "No."

Then notice a photograph hanging on the wall; it's a military photo, Marines to be exact.

"You're a Marine?" I ask.

He nods and takes a seat on the couch, "Yes ma'am, did a tour in Afghanistan."

"Wow, that's fascinating and scary," I say.

Brian laughs a bit before taking a sip of his wine, "Yeah, I guess those are two ways to describe it."

I smile and join him, resting my head on his chest as he puts his arm around me. We sit there for a moment in silence. I close my eyes, enjoying the music of his heart beating.

"Olivia?" Brian speaks.

"Yes?"

"Can you tell me what happened? Was he the person that gave you that black eye? Has he done this to you before?"

Every inch of my being wants to deny it and say no. But I can't, I'm tired of lying. I'm tired of hiding from this.

I take a deep breath and sit up, giving him my complete attention, "Yes. We were together for two years, and he physically abused me for the past year. Before you called me to tell me about my sister, he nearly killed me, but I fought back and got away."

Brian barely flinches at my revelation, "Did anyone else know?"

I look to my feet and shake my head, "No."

In fact, Brian is the only person that I can bring myself to admit this to.

"Not even your sister?" he asks.

"No, I was too ashamed to tell anyone, and...I kind of felt like I deserved it," I admit.

My hands are quivering again. I carefully reach for my wine glass and take another sip.

I can see that he's slightly perplexed at my words now, "Olivia, no woman deserves to be treated like that. You deserve a man that will give you the world, not one that will give you his fist. What if I hadn't shown up? Do you realize you could've died?"

I reach up, wiping the tears from my eyes, "Yes."

That evening, I lay in bed staring up at the ceiling. Brian is fast asleep beside me. Even though it felt good to finally open up to someone, I wish that I could talk to London and tell her everything that's been going on. I'd tell her how crazy my life has been without her and how I regret not taking advantage of the time we had together. I would tell her I was sorry for being distant and moving so far away.

Hours later, my phone rings with a new text. I grab it and nearly jump out of bed when I see who it is from.

**LONDON: YOU'RE GOING TO DIE...**

# LONDON

*Thursday, February 13, 2020*

I feel like I'm slipping off the edge. My head is spinning from confusion, frustration, and agonizing pain. I have no idea what I'm going to do. Memories of Chase just leaving replay in my mind. How could he just reject me like that? My mind races at how best to handle the situation.

*Would he even think the baby is his?*

*Is the baby his?*

*It has to be.*

Olivia would know what to do. I reach for my phone and dial her number. It's pretty late, hopefully she picks up. My heart sinks when it goes straight to voicemail.

*This is so fucked up.*

I hug my pillow tightly, crying until I fall asleep.

~

*Friday, February 14, 2020*

*I feel anxious. My heart is racing. I can't outrun him. I can feel him closing in on me. When he does, he grabs me by my hair. I try my hardest to fight him off, but my slaps and kicks do little to slow him down. Terrance's disgusting hands tightly close around my neck, making it nearly impossible to breathe. His cold, black eyes petrify me, sending chills down my spine. I try screaming, try finding Olivia, but she's nowhere in sight. The realization that my sister isn't here to protect me this time knocks the wind out of my chest. I panic; my heart races.*

~

I will myself to awaken from my nightmare. You know that eerie feeling when you know you're dreaming, but you can't seem to pull yourself out of it? Terrance has haunted my dreams quite a few times in my life, and it never gets any easier. My breathing is heavy and unsteady. My chest heaves, and I can feel my heart beating through my chest. I sense a heavy weight on my chest as if the sleep demon wants to keep me down, allowing Terrance to finish the job. The feeling is so strong, it makes me feel like I'm going to sink through my mattress and to the bottom of the earth.

*Wake up!*

Finally, I feel my eyes slowly peel open, my heart still racing. But as I come to, I feel hazy and dizzy. I instantly think about my baby. The thought of being a mother seems so foreign, but I can be enough for us. I have to be, regardless of whether or not Chase ever comes around.

A single candle casts a soft light throughout my bedroom. I stare up at my high ceiling, listening to the thundering rain outside. Suddenly, a chill creeps up my spine, and I feel uneasy, like someone is watching me. My eyes quickly scan the room; nothing seems to be out of place. Everything is exactly where I left it.

I take a few deep breaths, trying to calm my nerves, obviously still shaken up from my dream. I want to call my sister, but just as the thought crosses my mind, I see a dark object shift in the room.

There in the corner of my bedroom, stands a shadowy figure, moving closer and closer. I can't tell if this is real or if my mind is still playing tricks on me. I squint my eyes, trying to focus on what I think I'm seeing.

*Someone's here, this isn't a dream.*

*How long have they been here?*

*What do they want?*

I try to speak, but nothing comes out.

They slowly come forward, causing the hairs on the back of my neck to stand at attention. My eyes dart towards my bedroom door, and I try to calculate how fast I can make it past them and to safety. Just as I try to make a dash for it, my heart sinks when I see them run up beside me. They yank my hair and throw me down back onto the bed. Then I feel like I'm being electrocuted, and my body goes numb.

I can feel my adrenaline spike. I toss and turn in a frenzy, kicking and squirming, trying to fight my way free. But they close in, completely overpowering me.

I finally find my voice, "Who are you? Why are you doing this?"

Silence.

Then I feel it again, the sharp pain, and I'm slightly incapacitated again. I try to scream again for help, but their hand is over my mouth in an instant.

*I can't breathe.*

*I can't breathe!*

My eyes widen when I see the knife. Thoughts of my unborn child flash into my head, and I try fighting my way free. But they're too strong. Tears run down my face, then I feel the blade plunged deep into my chest.

The pain is indescribable, but I refuse to give up. I try to defend myself and my baby, but just as I do, I feel the sharp edge of the knife placed on my neck. Olivia pops into my head as I feel the flesh on my neck separate. It feels like I'm drowning. I gasp for air, but none fills my lungs. Then I see my attacker stand up, removing the mask from their face. I can't believe my eyes. I try to speak, to ask them why, but I feel myself slipping away.

# OLIVIA

R*ing!*
*Ring!*
*Ring!*
"Hello?" I answer.

"An inmate from a Pennsylvania correctional facility is trying to contact you. To accept the call please press one, to reject the call, please press two or hang up," the automated message recites.

I take a deep breath before pressing one.

"Hey mom," I say.

I can hear her sigh on the other end of the phone, "I didn't think you would answer."

"Why would you think that?"

"Because of the awful things I said to you when you came to see me. I'm so sorry ladybug, I was out of line. None of this is your fault," my mother cries.

I can feel my own tears forming, "You don't have anything to apologize for mom. I'm the one that should be apologizing. I was supposed to protect her, and I didn't. I should come and see you more but don't. I haven't been the best daughter. You've done so much for me."

My mother cries, "That's not true. I know that you feel guilty and you shouldn't. You protected your sister as best as you could baby and I am protecting you. I will continue to protect you until I take my last breath. Do you hear me?"

I sniff, "Yes."

She continues, "This is not on you. I know that you've carried this guilt around with you for a long time. You've got to let it go baby, it's eating you alive."

"I'm trying," I choke.

"You'll be alright, remember how strong you are, ok?" my mother says.

I nod to myself, I want to be strong again, I need to be.

~

Her apartment building looks so different these days. I used to love visiting my sister here. I always admired how elegant and cozy it was, but now as I look at it, the property feels evil and cold.

For some reason, I feel drawn to this place, London's place. That strange text is still bugging me. I made sure to show Brian as soon as we woke up this morning, and he assured me that he would look into it.

After leaving his place and talking to my mother, I find myself driving here. I walk inside and silently ride up the elevator.

I can feel my heart race as I near her door. But once there, I can't bring myself to go inside. I just stand there for a moment, trapped.

"Hi Olivia, is everything alright?"

Her voice startles me. I didn't even hear her approach.

"Hey, Shay, yes, I'm ok," I lie.

She glances at London's apartment door and then back to me, "How are you holding up?"

I shrug, "Just taking it day by day, you know. I won't be ok till they find this creep."

"I hope they do, and fast," she says. "Would you like to come by for some tea?"

I hesitate for a moment. I am really not in the mood to socialize, but I don't think I'm ready to go inside to Lon's place just yet. Maybe a cup of tea will help me calm my nerves.

"Yes, sure, thank you."

I follow Shay to her apartment door, and we walk inside.

"Have a seat, get comfortable," she says as she makes her way into the kitchen.

I do as I'm told and sit down. My eyes scan the room; it's not as clean as I would've expected.

"So, do the police have any new leads?" Shay calls out from the kitchen.

"No, not that I know of," I say.

I notice a magazine sitting on the coffee table and reach over to pick it up. When I do, a picture falls out. It's a picture of a man and woman, Shay. She looks younger and really happy. I quickly notice the huge diamond on her finger. I don't remember her mentioning that she was married before.

"Wow I didn't know that you were married. What happened to your husband?" I ask.

"Huh?"

I keep my eyes on the photo, "You were married, right?"

Suddenly, Avery's story pops back into my head.

*Something's not right.*

I turn it over and see the words 'Mike and Evelyn, 2012' scribbled on the back. My heart races as I put the photograph down and quietly reach for my keys. Just as I attempt to stand up off the couch, I feel a sharp pain in the nape of my neck. The bolt of electricity leaves me paralyzed. Before I can turn around, I feel a hard impact come across my head, causing me to blackout.

# OLIVIA

O*livia. You're going to die.*
*You have to wake up!*
*Don't let her kill you like she killed me!*

I come to and realize that my hands and feet are tied to rusty bedposts. I panic, trying to break myself free. My eyes quickly examine my surroundings, but the room is dimly lit.

I nearly choke when I see London. She's staring at me through twenty or so pictures hanging on the wall. The words slut and whore are spray painted over them in ruby red.

*What the fuck?*

I look around some more but can only make out a small dresser and a pile of dirty clothing tossed in the corner. Kelis' "Caught Out There" plays loudly through the small speaker across the room.

"Oh, you're awake!" Shay says as she enters.

"Shay, what the hell are you doing?" I yell.

She laughs sadistically, "Haven't you figured it out yet?"

The sudden realization that I was looking at my sister's killer sends chills down my spine.

"Why?" I cry.

"Why?" she laughs again. "Why?" She says once more with more conviction. "That slut had it coming! She ruined my life."

Just then, more details from Avery's tale about Shay's husband dying plays over in my head. Suddenly, I have this nagging feeling that the police's suspicions were right all along. However, none of that explains what this has to do with London.

"Ruined your life? How? I thought you two were friends."

Her skin is boiling red, "Friends? I despised that bitch. I could never be her friend! I only pretended to be so that I could get close to her and make her pay."

I cry, "Pay for what?"

"Your whore of a sister was sleeping with my husband. She seduced him with her games and convinced him that he didn't love me anymore, that's why," she fumes.

"You're crazy!"

Shay chuckles again, "Why does everyone keep saying that?"

Suddenly, Stormy's words pop into my head.

"You knew that girl, Stormy, didn't you?" I question.

She comes up to me and slaps me across my face with her free hand, "That's enough questions for now."

I notice the large knife and stun gun in her hands.

"You don't have to do this," I say.

"Well, since you like poking around, I figured what's one more dead body on my hands. The fact that you're her twin is a treat! It feels like I'm killing her all over again," she smiles and proceeds to poke me with the knife, leaving a small wound in my flesh.

My chest heaves.

"Playing tough, are we? My husband liked to play the tough guy too. He was so tough when he told me that he was leaving me for her, that was until I poisoned him. Can you believe that I actually got away with that? He just made me so angry, throwing away seven years of marriage for a dirty prostitute whore?" she snorts.

Angry tear drops escape my eyes.

She continues, "I wanted to kill Porsha, I mean London, the same night that I killed him, but I knew it would be hard to pull off. I mean, the police were hot on my tail for a while. So, I waited and planned for the perfect time to strike. First off, I got rid of that bitch friend of hers, Inez. She was becoming a nuisance and pain in my side. I knew that if I allowed her to get close to London again, she'd fill her head with foolishness about me. So, I trapped her. I used my key and snuck into London's apartment while she was fast asleep and sent Inez a text from her phone asking her to meet me out."

"You have a key to London's apartment?" I sob.

Shay nods, visibly proud of herself and her well-thought-out operation, "Piece of cake, really. I tricked her into finishing my laced drink. When she blacked out, who else but her nice neighbor was going to drive her home and make sure she'd be safe? I couldn't kill her that night like I had initially planned. Too many people saw me leave with her. It was a shame, really. But while she was basically comatose, I had a key made, convinced her that her best friend drugged her and then I waited for the perfect time to strike. She never saw me coming, ha!"

Now my skin is on fire. My rage is boiling over, and I feel like I'm going to explode.

She continues, "Anyway, back to that bitch, Inez. I had her meet me at this fancy hotel. Stayed hidden in the shadows, like that day you saw me on the running trail. Then I pushed that cunt right over the balcony."

My head reels with all of this information. I've hugged this girl and tried being nice to her. She was at my sister's funeral; she'd been so close this entire time and had everyone fooled.

"London was so consumed with her own pathetic life and that man she fell in love with. When I heard that he was married, I decided enough was enough. She would not do this to another woman, not anymore. So while she was asleep, I snuck into her apartment and made sure of just that."

The song starts over.

"You know, this is my favorite song? I used to play it over and over as I imagined how I would kill your sister," Shay giggles.

She is angry and thirsty for more blood, my blood. I pull on my arms, hoping to get the restraints loose like I did when I was held captive by Marcus. But these are different, and much more difficult to manipulate.

*Think, Olivia, think!*

She sits down beside me, "And don't think that Chase is off the hook. Who do you think tipped the police off? I just didn't expect his wife to cover for him; that definitely was not a part of the plan," she admits.

"You're not going to get away with this, Evelyn," I say.

She winces at the sound of her real name.

"Evelyn is gone; she was weak and just pitiful! I'm Shay now. I'm strong, and I fear no one, not my husband, not your sister, and definitely not you, bitch!" she snaps.

I can see her veins popping out through her neck, her hand gripped tightly around the handle of the blade. She presses the sharp edge firmly against my throat. I close my eyes, trying to anticipate the pain. Suddenly, there's a knock at the front door.

"Dammit," she says, frustrated.

Shay stuffs an old rag in my mouth and puts the knife and stun gun on top of the dresser. I watch in terror as she heads into the living room to answer the door.

I toss and turn and try my best to make noise.

"Yes, detective?" she says when she answers the door.

My heart races.

"Is this a bad time?"

The sound of Brian's voice shoots a jolt of adrenaline throughout my body. I have to get free.

"Actually it is; what's this about?" Shay says.

As I listen to them talk, I continue to pull on my restraints. I bite my lip at the pain of my skin rubbing against the fabric until my hand finally comes undone.

"It seems that we traced a signal from London Burrows' phone to your residence this morning," Brian explains.

As soon as he says the words, I am in complete shock. He assured me that he would have his team look into it, and I'm so happy that they came through. I can't believe just how sick and sadistic Shay is. I reach up, quickly releasing my other hand before ripping the cloth out of my mouth.

"Brian! I'm in here! Help!" I scream out.

"Freeze!" Andrews shouts before the front door slams shut.

The sound of a table being dragged across the floor rings out. Then I hear her angry footsteps draw closer towards the bedroom. I undo my ankles and stand to my feet.

Just as she bursts back into the room, she rushes towards the dresser to retrieve the knife. But before she can, I tackle her with all my might, slamming her into the floor.

"You fucking bitch!" she sneers.

She rips at my hair and I tug on hers, scratching and punching what I can. I can hear Brian in the background trying to burst the door down. Part of me wants to run out of this place and to safety, but I'm tired of running. Shay has to pay for what she's done.

We toss around on the floor, trying to tear one another to shreds. I can feel her overpowering me and quickly use my leg to push her off my body. As I do, she crashes into the dresser, causing the knife and stun gun to fall to the floor. I try to hop up as fast as I can, but I'm too late, I feel the bolt of electricity again causing me to fall face first to the ground once more.

Shay is out of breath, but she doesn't let up. I feel her arms tug on my body, rolling me over onto my back. I try to fight her off, but she stuns me again. She climbs on top of me, holding my arms down with her knees, and places the blade to my throat.

"Nice try bitch," she says.

"Ma'am, drop the knife!" Brian commands as he charges through the room.

He's astonished to see photographs of London all over the place.

"Or what? Are you going to kill me?" Shay challenges him, pressing the knife deeply into my skin, slightly cutting me.

I flinch at the pain and can feel the blood dripping down my throat.

Brian holds steady, "Back-up is already on the way. Put the knife down, and step away from the girl. This is your last warning."

Shay shakes her head, furious, "You've ruined everything!"

Suddenly, she lifts her arm high in the air, preparing to stab me.

*Bang!*

She falls down beside me, blood splattering from her wound and onto the dirty floor. Brian rushes over to us, first kicking the knife from her hand and then reaching down to check her pulse.

He sighs, "She's dead."

Brian helps me up in an instant, his eyes eagerly searching for any wounds or damage. I see him relax when he realizes that I'm relatively unharmed. I am eager to be in his arms and hug him tightly. I can feel his heart is racing like mine.

"You saved me again; you're like my own personal superman," I say.

"I'm up for the task," he replies.

Without hesitating, I kiss him with complete passion. I don't know if it is the brush with death or my angst. I just have to feel him.

When we pull away, Brian smiles, "I guess that means thank you."

I nod and lick my lips, "It does; take me home."

In the hallway, I can hear the police calling out to Brian.

*I guess that will have to wait.*

I turn around, about to leave the bedroom but stop to get one last look at Shay. Her chest is open from the single gunshot wound. Her eyes are still open, staring at me.

*It's finally over.*

*Four months later...*

My phone vibrates, and I check my phone.

**BRIAN: DINNER AT MY PLACE TONIGHT? I HOPE YOU LIKE ITALIAN ;-)**

**OLIVIA: IT'S A DATE.**

I blush and promptly put my phone away, opting to pick up a magazine off the glass top coffee table. Minutes later, the door opens, and my new therapist, Dr. Jacqueline Nelson enters the room. I watch as she takes a seat in the chair facing me and admire her Christian Louboutin heels.

She greets me, "How are you doing this week, Olivia?"

"I'm doing fine," I smile.

Dr. Nelson is poised and looks better than the headshot photo on her website. Before I found her, I spent weeks trying to find the perfect therapist. According to Yelp, this lady knows her stuff and helps people overcome all types of trauma. Let's just say, Jacqueline Nelson is the best of the best. If I had to guess, she is in her late forties but could easily pass for late twenties.

I toss the magazine back down onto the table. The office is warm and welcoming, just how I like it, adorned with soft blues, cream backgrounds, and gold accents. There's got to be a gazillion books in here. The faint smell of vanilla and jasmine tickle my nose. I softly smile to myself.

*London.*

"So, you've been coming to see me for the last three months, and I am impressed with the progress you've made," Jacqueline says.

I have spent the last few weeks sorting through all of what has happened since my return to Philadelphia: from losing my sister to my mother being in prison, the attack from Marcus and then Shay. Coming to terms with my past and processing my feelings about the new realities of my life have been a journey.

Avery was gracious enough to hire me as her assistant. It may not be as glamorous as owning my own company, but I really like what I do, and for the first time in a long time, I feel inspired to do something with my life. I can credit my new relationship with Brian for my new attitude. He makes me feel like a new woman. I feel safe and excited for what the future holds, especially with us. Therapy is everything that I never knew that I needed. It feels so good to talk about these things and get them out, good and bad, well almost.

"Olivia?" she says, bringing me back to reality.

"Huh?"

"I was saying that I'm happy with your progress, but I feel like something is holding you back from completely healing. You seem to have a complex relationship with your sister and mother. I'd like to explore that today."

I nervously nibble on my nail and tap my foot unsure of what to say.

"How about you tell me more about your sister, London?"

Dr. Nelson leans back into her seat, crossing her legs, waiting for me to begin.

She is right; something is holding me back.

London's killer has been found.

I've reconnected with my mother.

Marcus is rotting in jail and completely out of my life for good.

All those things, and I still feel off.

"Her murder wasn't your fault, you understand that, right?" she says, interrupting my thoughts once more.

I shake my head no, "I should've been there for her."

"How does that make you feel?"

"Angry," I confess.

"What else?"

"Frustrated, helpless."

"Why?" she pries.

"My sister was infamous for putting me in situations that made me uncomfortable. I always felt like I had to clean up her mess. It was my job to protect her," I confess.

Dr. Nelson leans forward a smidge in her chair, intrigued, "Why? Why do you feel like you had to protect her?"

"Because I always have," I say.

"I see," she says. "Do you feel that your propensity to always clean up your sister's messes has benefited your life in any way?"

I shake my head, "No."

"Interesting. Was there another time in your lives where you had to protect her?"

I nod.

"Do you feel like sharing today? I think getting to the root of this will take a lot of the emotional weight you've been carrying off of your shoulders."

I want to tell her. I want to share my truth, the whole truth, but I'm scared.

*What if she turns me in to the police?*

It's like she can sense my question, "Remember, anything you say in here stays in here between you and me. I'm only obligated to report what you say if I feel that you're a threat to yourself or others."

"Do you think that I am a threat?"

She leans towards me, "No. I think that you're just carrying a lot of trauma and guilt about your sister. That's understandable. You were twins. I can imagine how deep your bond was. Wanting to protect her is absolutely normal."

I start to cry, "I'd kill for her."

"Many people feel that way about the ones they love," she nods.

"But I actually did."

I hold my breath for a long spell, waiting for the judgment to come, but it never does.

"It's ok," she encourages.

"My mother, she had the worst taste in men. Especially when it came to Terrance. He was a sick bastard. He was raping London and got her pregnant. She made me promise not to tell," I cry.

Part of me feels guilty for telling her dirty secret now, but these secrets have eaten me alive. I know that in order to get my life back, I have to come clean to someone.

"I went with her to get an abortion. They wouldn't let me in the room with her. She needed me!" I cry.

Dr. Nelson hands me tissues, and I grab one, wiping my eyes.

I take a deep breath and continue, "Later that night, our mom went to work, and Terrance went to her room. Something in me snapped. I knew that he would never stop hurting her. So I went into my mother's bedroom and got her gun out of her nightstand."

The memories play out in my mind as if it were yesterday.

"I walked in as he was touching her. His pants were down, and she was crying. I had to protect her," I say. "Out of nowhere, my mom came home. Apparently, they were overstaffed that night, and she got the night off. She walked in as Terrance was standing there with his dick out, begging for forgiveness. She begged me to put the gun down. I almost did, but I wanted him to confess. But then he reached and tried grabbing London. I panicked. I couldn't let him touch her," I cry, letting the weight and the guilt of this secret spill out.

Jacqueline joins me on the couch, tenderly rubbing my back.

"My mom called the cops and turned herself in. She took the blame for it all," I say.

"She was protecting you like you were protecting your sister," Dr. Nelson says.

I sniff, "Yeah, I know that now. I just feel so guilty. I should be in jail, not her."

"Your mother made a choice. Maybe this was her way to make amends, for failing to protect you both from a predator," she explains.

I never looked at it that way.

"So, where do you go from here?" Jacqueline asks.

I sit, pondering her question for a moment.

*Where do I go from here?*

Thanks to London making me her beneficiary, I don't have to worry about money for a while.

"I want to help women that were abused like me. Maybe I can go back to school so that I can be a therapist like you," I finally say.

She nods, "That's a great idea, Olivia."

I grin, because deep down I know that it is.

~

The summer breeze is cool and refreshing. I keep my eyes on the brick house, anxiously waiting for his arrival. A few minutes later, I see a black Jaguar pull into the driveway. Before I can change my mind, I hop out of my car and hurry across the street, nearing the house.

He's hunched over in his trunk, grabbing grocery bags. I take slow and deliberate steps, trying to decide the best way to approach him. Once he gathers his things, he swiftly closes the trunk and heads towards his home.

"You just going to stand there?" Chase says over his shoulder.

I watch him as he lets himself into the residence, leaving the door cracked. I'll admit, once I knew who Chase really was, it wasn't hard to track him down. Since his arrest and release, he'd been a hot topic buzzing through the news headlines for a few months. I guess the hot teacher bedding his former student and possibly killing her was a reporter's dream. Too bad for them that Chase was, in fact, innocent and wrongly accused, apparently set-up by Shay.

The house is modern but a bit disorderly. There are a ton of books and magazines, along with old tennis shoes and a bicycle by the entrance. I gently close the door behind me and weave my fingers together. Moments later, Chase comes in holding two glasses of lemonade.

"I figured you'd like something to drink. It was pretty humid today," he says.

*And answers.*

I nod and take a seat near him on the couch as he places our drinks down. Chase's face looks tired, strained. It's safe to say, the man's been put through the wringer.

He sighs, "I know why you're here. I figured you'd find me eventually."

"Why did you avoid me all those times before?" I ask.

He sighs, "Isn't that obvious?"

I shake my head, confused.

Chase carefully sips his drink, "Because every time that I would see you, it was like I was seeing your sister."

"I thought it was because you killed her."

"No. Because I was, and still am, having a hard time accepting that she's no longer alive," he admits.

I say, "The cops said you were the last person to see her before she died. What happened?"

He sighs again, "We had a fight the night before. I found out about her, err, lifestyle, and I just couldn't handle it. She discovered that I'm in the process of getting a divorce, and it was all a bit too much, honestly. I was in a really bad headspace and needed someone to talk to. I stupidly went over to my ex-wife's house and ended up passing out on her couch that night. That obviously saved my life."

"I'd say so," I reply.

Chase nods, "I tried keeping my distance, but I couldn't. So, I went over to her place a couple nights later to talk. She wasn't answering any of my texts or calls."

Suddenly, Chase gets a bit choked up.

"Her door was unlocked," he finally says. "I walked inside and saw her lying there, already dead."

I can't stop myself from crying.

He shakes his head, "I panicked and left. Once I got to my car, I called 911."

Chase puts his head in his hands, clearly tormented.

After a long moment, he looks me squarely in the eyes, "I would've never hurt your sister. I love her."

"Did you know?" I ask.

"About?"

My voice trembles, "The pregnancy."

He shakes his head again, putting his fingers into his tear ducts to stop from crying, "Not until the detectives told me."

I take a sip of my lemonade.

Chase continues, "I just hate that I wasn't there to protect her."

"It's not your fault," I say, placing the glass down.

He stands, pacing before me, "If we hadn't had that fight, she wouldn't have been alone that night."

"If you were there, you both would have gotten killed," I reason.

He's indifferent. I can tell he will likely never see it that way. I know a thing or two about guilt, so I understand.

"How are you holding up?" he asks.

I shrug, "Taking it day by day, I guess."

Chase bows his head with understanding, "Your sister was very bright, one of the most interesting women I've ever met in my life."

I smile. I can tell that Chase is genuine with every word he's saying. He loved my sister very much; he still does.

I stand, "Thank you for talking to me, and you know, telling me the truth."

"You're welcome," he says.

I grab my purse and rise from the couch. Chase leads me to the door, opening it.

"I want you to know that I really do love your sister. I was a coward," he reveals.

"I know that you love her. Don't be so hard on yourself," I reply.

Chase nods, trying to heed to my words. I watch him put his hands into his pockets and lightly kick at the ground.

"I guess I'll see you around," I say.

He looks up at me, "I promise that I won't avoid you next time."

We share a broken laugh.

"Take care," I say.

"You too."

As I step out onto his porch, I see the sun is setting. I take a deep breath and inhale the warm summer air. For the first time in a long time, it feels good to be home. Inside my car, I adjust my rearview mirror before pulling out into the evening traffic. I drive down the busy street, leaving my past and the girl that I was in the distance and driving towards my future and the woman that I am finally ready and eager to become.

The End

*Coming Soon...*

*Stormy*

I get out of my BMW, leaving my keys with the valet attendant. Earlier this morning, I received an intriguing email from a potential client. They were eager to meet me and made it clear they would make it worth my while.

Upon entering Barclay Prime, I'm greeted by a warm hostess.

"Hello, how can I help you, miss?"

"I'm meeting someone under the name Preston."

She nods and says, "Right this way."

I follow her through the restaurant towards a table nestled in the back corner. To my surprise, a woman is seated at the table, sipping a cocktail, waiting for me.

"Preston?" I say.

She nods, "Yes."

I take my seat with curiosity.

"You look like you've seen a ghost," she says.

"No, I'm just confused; that's all."

"Don't be. Have a seat. I'll explain everything," she coolly says.

I sit down in the chair, eyeing her with caution. She's very attractive, a little older but still a looker. I notice her perfectly manicured nails and diamond earrings. She definitely has money. Before either of us can say another word, the waiter approaches our table.

"I'll have a dirty martini please," I say.

"Same for me."

He quickly nods, leaving us to talk.

She smiles and crosses her fingers, "How is business treating you?"

"Business is good, but it could always be better," I taunt.

*This bitch is baiting me.*

I keep my cool and play into her game.

"You're breathtakingly beautiful. I'm sure you can get any guy that you want," she replies.

*Ok, now she's being condescending.*

Before I can snap on her, the waiter returns with our drinks, placing each one down in front of us. As he leaves, I opt to get straight to the point. I've become irritated with the games.

"Ok, you got me here, so cut to the chase. What do you want?" I say.

She smiles before picking up her martini and taking a sip.

As she puts her drink back down on the table, she looks deep into my eyes, "I want you to sleep with my husband."

# MORE BOOKS BY MONIQUE

Are you looking for a new book (or three) to fall in love with? Three friends, three love stories, one EPIC series! Get to know Jade: The heart-breaker, Blair: The woman scorned and Kara: The hopeless romantic. Are you a Jade, Blair, or Kara? Grab some wine and get to know each character and their riveting stories! "Dilemmas of a Damsel" is a provocative tale that is jam-packed with romance, drama, and plenty of scandal! Available on Amazon and Kindle Unlimited.

# ABOUT THE AUTHOR

Monique Elise is well on her way to becoming a household name. A self-proclaimed glow-getter, Monique is passionate about telling stories that highlight black and brown love while using her imagination to connect with her readers in a meaningful way. She is most widely regarded for her racy debut series, Dilemmas of a Damsel. To learn more about Monique and her work, please visit www.MoniqueElise.com.

## Connect with Monique

 @Author Monique Elise

 @moniqueelise__

 @iammoniqueelise

 @Monique Elise

 **hello@moniqueelise.com**

Join my mailing list at www.moniqueelise.com for all the latest news, giveaways, and exclusive sneak peeks!

If you liked this book, please leave a review on Amazon and Goodreads!

Made in the USA
Middletown, DE
20 June 2020